Published by Lakisha Johnson | Twins Write 2 Publishing

Edition License Notes

This book is licensed for your personal enjoyment only. This book may not be re-sold or given away to other people. If you would like to share this book with another person, please purchase an additional copy for each recipient.

If you're reading this book and did not purchase it, or it was not purchased for your enjoyment only, then please return to your favorite retailer and purchase your own copy. Thank you for respecting the hard work of this author.

The Marriage Bed

Dedication

This book is dedicated to my husband of twenty-years, Willie Johnson.

Being with you hasn't always been easy but man, it sure has been worth it. Thank you *"husbae"* for always supporting, putting up with my attitude, my never-ending work schedule, ministry, writing and everything else.

You share me with people, every day and although you complain, sometimes, you know everything I do is to retire us sooner than later.

I love you and look forward to many more years of love, laughter and living.

The Johnsons | May 2, 1998

The Marriage Bed

My Gratefulness

As always, I owe all to God. Without His anointing, I would not be able to give you the books you so graciously purchase, release after release.

I thank my husband, Willie for being so gracious to share me with each of you. My children Gabrielle and Christopher, my mom, sisters, brothers, cousins and friends. I love each of you!

To you, the readers who continually support Lakisha, from every chamber of my heart … THANK YOU! Without you purchasing, reading, reviewing and recommending; my books would never make it to be best sellers. YOU GUYS ROCK!

Please don't stop supporting me!

The Marriage Bed

Lies and Deception

The Marriage Bed

July 15, 2000

"Congratulations Mrs. Watson." I say when she rolls off me.

"Congratulations Mr. Watson." She pants.

"Thank you for making me the happiest man alive."

"Are you truly happy Jerome?" She asks.

"Why would you ask me that? Of course, I am."

"We just graduated college, got a baby due in four weeks, living in a one-bedroom basement apartment and a car that's barely hanging on."

"So!" I say rolling over to look at her. "Lynn Nicole Watson, you are the only person for me and you make me the happiest I've ever been. I don't care if we were living in a cardboard box, as long as I have you girl." I sing.

"You say that now."

She gets up. "Babe, it's just your hormones. Come and lay down."

"Will you promise me something Jerome?"

"Anything babe, just stop crying."

"Will you promise to talk to me if you ever get the desire to cheat?" She asks.

I laugh. She doesn't.

"Wait, are you serious?"

She walks out the room.

"Where are you going?"

I hear her rummaging through newspaper before she comes back with a bible in her hand. She plops back down on the bed.

"Babe--" She holds up one finger.

"The bible says in Hebrews 13:4, "Let marriage be held in honor among all, and let the marriage bed be undefiled, for God will judge the sexually immoral and adulterous." She reads.

"What does that mean?"

"Marriage bed means sexual relations between husband and wife. So, this is saying we should never violate the purity of our marriage bed by cheating and lying." She states. "Jerome, I plan on being with you for the rest of my life, but I am not crazy. I know you will desire other women

but promise, if you ever get the taste for something, other than what I serve, you'll tell me."

"Babe this is our marriage, not a buffet. I married you because I love, honor and cherish you. If I wanted other women, I'd be with them. This is crazy and ruining our wedding night."

"I am not trying to do that, but I am being realistic in knowing, fifteen years from now your mouth may desire something other than me. Let me be clear, I am not giving you open access to cheat, but I don't want our marriage bed tainted. All you have to do is talk to me first. Promise?" She asks holding out her pinky finger.

"What if I do tell you then what?"

"Then we decide what to do next but whatever we do, we do it together, in our marriage bed and on one accord."

"You're serious?"

"So serious. We've been together, already, for five years and we're only twenty-two with no other sexual partners or experiences and before you hurt me, I'd rather be safe than sorry."

She holds out her pinky. "Promise me."

"Okay," I say locking mine with hers. "Now, come back to bed woman."

Lynn

Present Day

I run around the bedroom, lighting the candles on the nightstand. When I hear the chirp of the alarm, I quickly turn off the lights, remove my robe and stand next to the bed.

"Lynn, where are you?" Jerome calls out.

"In the bedroom."

"Why do you have the lights off?" He asks flicking the light switch and then laughing. "What are you doing and what do you have on?"

"I am trying to have a romantic night with my husband." I angrily reply grabbing my robe.

"Why are you dressed like a street walker? Where are the kids?" He asks taking off his suit jacket and throwing it across the chair.

"They are with my parents for the weekend but just disregard the fact your wife is standing in front of you semi-nude." I reply blowing out the candles. "What is wrong with you?"

"Me? What is wrong with you? Where did you even get that outfit from?"

"I bought it because I thought you'd appreciate me going out of my way."

"Why would you think that? I just hope nobody saw you in the store." He says.

"Because I am your wife and it's the only thing I requested for my birthday."

His eyes widen.

"You forgot. Figures."

"Babe, I'm sorry." He says sitting on the side of the bed. "With everything going on at work and the church, it slipped my mind. We had the final meeting with the new youth minister and she accepted the position. I think she's going to be a great fit for the church and the changes with the youth department and you're going to like her, I think. In fact, you both kind of favor."

"JEROME!" I yell to stop him from speaking. "I don't want to talk about no freaking church when I'm standing here half naked."

"Sorry. Look, put some clothes on, some *decent* clothes and we can go out to eat."

"No," I say slowly walking up to him. "I have everything we need right here so why don't you take off your clothes and we stay in?" I kiss him on the forehead before loosening his tie. "I went to this store and got some stuff for us to play with and," I kiss him again.

"What kind of stuff?" He asks interrupting.

"Some edible stuff." I kiss him again. "Some sticky stuff." I kiss him again. "And some kinky, useful stuff."

"Wait, you mean them sex toys?"

"Yep and whip cream, strawberries--"

He pushes me away.

"You know I'm not using those things Lynn."

I fall onto the bed. "Come on Jerome. What's the harm? It's our marriage bed and the bible says--"

"I know what the bible says but aren't you the one who just said you didn't want to hear not bible talk?"

"You know that is not what I meant. We need some fun added to our marriage bed."

"There is nothing wrong with our marriage bed. We have three children to prove that and if it ain't broke, don't break it trying to fix it."

"Jerome, making children has nothing to do with our sex life which sucks, by the way."

"Where are you getting this from? Who have you been talking too?"

"Why would I need to talk to anybody? If you were to get your head out of the bible and look at your wife, you'd see for yourself. All we ever do, is the same old tired missionary position with your five pumps. Hell, your idea of foreplay is rubbing on me like we're in middle school. You don't even kiss me anymore and I'm tired of it. I want you to make love to me like you used too!"

"You been watching that Fifty Shades stuff again, haven't you? What did I tell you about that mess? Got you around here looking and sounding like a plum fool."

"Forget you Jerome!"

"Lynn, I don't know what is wrong with you but I'm going to take a shower. If you want to go out to dinner, be dressed by the time I am done."

He walks into the bathroom and slams the door.

I walk into the closet and take off the lingerie and slip on a bra. I look through my clothes and pull a black tank dress from the hanger.

Putting it on, I grab a pair of black strappy sandals from the shelf. Sitting on the ottoman, I fasten them before standing to look at myself in the full-length mirror.

I run my hand over my hair and look closely to ensure my makeup is still intact. I take a red clutch from the shelf before leaving out the bedroom and going into the kitchen to get my license, lip gloss, credit card and keys from my other purse.

Making sure I have everything, I walk over to the alarm panel. Setting it to stay, I open the door before turning to look down the hall.

"Oh, I got your dinner boo."

Jerome

"Babe, where do you want to go for dinner? Babe."

When she doesn't answer, I figure she is still mad, so I shrug and begin singing.

"Jesus is on the main line, tell him what you want. Oh, Jesus is on the main line, tell him what you want. Jesus is on the main line, tell him what you want. Call him up and tell him what you want."

I turn off the water and dry off, wrapping the towel around my waist. I open the door, "Lynn?"

I walk to the dresser, grab a pair of boxers pull them on and walk into the closet. I stop when I see the outfit Lynn had on in the closet floor. I put on a pair of jeans and a t-shirt before turning off the light and heading up front to see where she is.

"Babe, where do you want to eat?"

I look up to see the living room empty. I walk into the kitchen. "Lynn?"

I walk throughout the house and she's not here.

Going back into the bedroom, I pick up my phone from the nightstand and dial her number.

No answer.

I dial it again.

No answer.

I send a text.

ME: Lynn, where are you?

After a few minutes, no response.

I call our oldest daughter, Lilly who is almost eighteen.

"Hey dad, what's up?"

"Hey, have you heard from your mom?" I question.

"Not since earlier when I called to wish her a Happy Birthday. Why?"

"She isn't answering her phone."

"Dad, what did you do?" She asks.

Silence.

"You forgot her birthday again, didn't you?"

More silence.

"Dang daddy! I sent you a text and told you not to forget."

"I know and I'm sorry, but I got busy at the office."

She blows. "I am not the one you should be apologizing too." She states. "I'll call her."

"God no. Please don't do that because I'd never hear the end of it."

She laughs.

"Okay but daddy, you know you messed up, right?"

"I know."

I hang up from her and try to call Lynn again, but she still doesn't answer.

Sighing and cursing under my breath, I lay back on the bed with the phone in my hand, deciding to try her again in a few minutes.

Lynn

"Good evening and welcome to The Underground. My name is KJ, your attendant for the evening. What can I get you to drink?"

"Um, I'll take a mojito."

"Can I see your id please?" He asks.

"Sure." I get it from my clutch and hand it to him.

"Happy Birthday." He says smiling.

"Thank you."

"Here is the food menu and I'll be right back with your drink."

When he walks off, I pull out my phone to see a few missed calls and a text message from Jerome. I clear them before opening Facebook. Scrolling through my timeline, I start to like and comment on some of the Happy Birthday posts.

"I hear it's your birthday."

I look up to see whose speaking and my eyes travel the lengths of his gorgeous frame.

"It is." I reply.

"Well, your drinks are on the house tonight." He says handing me my mojito.

"You don't have to do that."

"Of course I do because tonight, you're my VIP guest. Would you like something to eat? Our wings are delicious."

"Well then, I'll take an order of your delicious wings." I smile.

"Great. If there is anything and I do mean anything you need, let KJ know and he or I will take care of it."

Before I can reply, he walks off. I smile taking a sip from my drink.

I put the phone in my purse and begin swaying to the music.

"Lynn?"

I turn to the sound of someone calling my name.

"Mattie, hey, what are you doing here?"

"Meeting some friends. What are you doing here?" She asks, eyeing me suspiciously.

"Celebrating my birthday."

"Okay girl. Where is Jerome?"

"At home."

She looks surprised.

"What?" I ask.

"Nothing, I'm just surprised to see you here. I never took this for your kind of hang out."

"Well, it's not but I saw it on Facebook and since my husband forgot my birthday, I decided to give it a try."

"He forgot your birthday? Well, forget him with his old peanut head ass."

"I plan on it." I laugh.

"Not by yourself, I hope. Why don't you come join me and my friends?"

"No, I wouldn't want to intrude."

"Nonsense. Come on." She says grabbing my arm.

When we walk up to a table with three other women, I try not to show my nervousness.

"Ladies!" Mattie sings, walking up to the table.

"It's about time, where have you been?" One of the girls ask Mattie, clearly annoyed.

"Handling grown folk business. Anyway, this is Lynn, a friend and church member." She announces.

"Church member and you're inviting here to hang with us?" The same chick asks.

"Erica, chill. She's cool people plus today is her birthday too."

"Happy Birthday." The other two say together.

"What are you drinking?" Mattie asks.

"A mojito."

"Oh no, you need a real drink." She says taking it from my hand. "I'll be right back."

I try to protest but Mattie is gone before I can part my lips.

"You can sit here." The mouthy chick says removing her jacket. "I'm Erica, this is Tasha and that one over there is Bea, the other birthday girl."

"Hi ladies. Thank you for letting me crash your party and happy birthday Bea."

"If Mattie says you're cool people, you must be." Tasha says.

"Lynn, how old are you?" Bea asks.

"40."

"40!" Erica says choking on her drink. "Damn, you look good."

"Thank you." I state, blushing.

"Are you married?"

"I am."

"And your husband let you out the house looking like this? Baby, you over there looking like a whole snack."

"Thank you, I think." I reply laughing.

They laugh.

"Okay ladies let's get this party started." Mattie says dancing up to the table with KJ who has my wings.

She hands me a small glass before passing the others to the ladies.

"What's this?" I inquire.

Bea passes a salt shaker around and we pour some on the back of our hands.

"Don't ask just drink." She says. "To many more years of joyful birthdays."

We all clink glasses, down the drink, lick the salt and then suck the lime.

I close my eyes as the liquid goes down.

"You'll get the hang of it." Mattie says laughing before sitting next to Erica who she kisses on the lips.

I cannot lie, I blushed a little.

When Mattie comes up for air, she looks at me and smiles.

I return the smile before grabbing a wing.

After hours of drinking, more shots, eating and dancing, I leave the girls on the dance floor to find the bathroom. I stagger and laugh before pushing open the door. I walk into the stall and lift my dress.

When I'm done, I flush and open the door. Taking a step out, someone pushes me back in.

"What the—Mattie? What are you doing?"

"Shush." She says rubbing her finger across my lips, dragging it down my chin then in between my breasts.

"I can't do this. It's wrong," I slur.

"Who's going to stop us?" She asks covering my ear with her mouth.

I close my eyes. "Hmm," I moan.

The door to the bathroom opens.

"Shit." We hear Bea say. "I wonder where Mattie and Lynn went."

My eyes fly open but Mattie only smiles.

Mattie pulls her dress up. "Lift your legs." She mouths.

I wrap my legs around her waist. She turns to sit on the toilet.

"I don't know." Erica states. "I'm going to call her."

"I'm in here." Mattie answers. "That liquor messed with my stomach."

"Are you okay? You need me to get you a ginger ale?" Erica asks her.

"Yea but take it to the table and I'll be out." She says, her hand sliding under my dress. I quickly cover my mouth to keep any sound from escaping as my eyes get bigger when I feel her fingers touch my lady.

"Where is Lynn?" Erica asks.

She slides a finger into me and I have to bite my lip.

"Um, she left."

"Are you sure you're okay?" Erica asks.

"Yes, just give me a few minutes."

A few seconds later, we hear the toilet flush, then the water turn on and finally the door opens and closes.

Mattie is staring into my eyes.

When her fingers begin to move inside of me, for a second I enjoy the feeling but then I move from her lap.

Pressing my back against the door, I push my dress down. Catching my breath, I shake my head to gather my thoughts. "I, we cannot do this. I'm sorry."

I open the door and rush out of the bathroom.

Instead of going back the way I came, I take another way to the front of the club. I get inside my car and lock the doors before pressing the start button.

My phone vibrates with a text from Mattie.

MATTIE: I'm sorry if I made you feel uncomfortable.

ME: You didn't. You made me feel wanted.

MATTIE: I'm here if you need me. Text me when you get home.

Reaching into the door of the car, I grab some napkins and wipe between my legs. I ball them up tightly and as I pull off, I let the window down and throw them out.

Making the thirty-minute trip home, I am overloaded by my thoughts. I finally pull in the garage. Before getting out, I lay my head on the headrest and say a quick prayer of forgiveness.

I turn the car off, grab my purse and head inside, letting the garage down.

Jerome

I jump up when I hear the alarm chirp, realizing I'd fallen asleep with the phone in my hand. I walk down the hall and turn into the kitchen at the same time Lynn closes the refrigerator, causing her to jump.

"Where have you been?" I yell.

"You scared me."

"Where have you been?" I ask again.

"Out." She replies opening the bottle of water and drinking the entire thing.

"You went out dressed like that?"

"Yep."

"Where did you go?"

"Out."

"Out where?" I question getting agitated.

"Somewhere to celebrate my birthday seeing it didn't mean anything to you." She says brushing by me.

"You know that is not true." I reply grabbing her arm. "Wait, have you been drinking?"

"Yep."

She snatches her arm from me and turns to walk down the hall.

"Hold on!"

"What Jerome?"

"What in the hell has gotten into you!"

"Are you cursing at me?" She giggles. "Well daddy, nothing has gotten into me. I went out to celebrate my birthday because it's apparent you had no intention of doing so because you've yet to even say happy birthday."

"Lynn, I get you're upset but stop overreacting."

"How am I overreacting?"

"First, look at this room. You have candles everywhere, you spent money on all kinds of stuff I'd never use and now you're out in public dressed like this and drinking! What if someone from the church saw you?" I yell.

"Stop yelling." She says, sitting on the side of the bed.

"I am going to ask you for the final time. Where have you been?"

"Out." She replies while typing on her phone.

"Who are you texting?" I question snatching it from her and reading the texts.

HER: Hey Mattie, thank you for tonig

"Is this Mattie from the church?"

"Yep."

"What are you thanking her for?"

She doesn't respond and instead finishes the text, locks the phone and begins removing her shoes.

"You were hanging out with Mattie?"

"Yep."

"Lynn, I swear to God if you say yep one more time."

"What are you going to do Jerome? Huh? I am not your child and I could really care less about what you're saying, right now."

"Is that so? Then tell me what you've been doing?"

"FOR THE LAST FREAKING TIME, I'VE BEEN CELEBRATING MY BIRTHDAY!"

"Why couldn't you do that with me? I offered to take you out to eat." I say matter-of-factly.

"Man, you can shove that dinner up your a--"

"LYNN!"

"WHAT? Are you going to tell me I can't say the word ass? Why not? Will God condemn me? Will I be cast to hell?" She asks sarcastically. "Ass, ass, ass."

"Who are you because my wife would not come waltzing in at 1:30am, dressed like you work at a strip club and smelling like alcohol."

"My name is Lynn Watson and I am a fed up wife." She says extending her hand. "It's nice to meet you."

"Fed up?" I laugh. "I guess you learned that while you were out lollygagging with Mattie, of all people."

"What is that supposed to mean? Of all people."

"Oh, don't act like you haven't heard the rumors around church. Everybody knows she's a lesbian."

"And?"

"And you have no business being with her."

"Why not?" She asks crossing her arms. "Please tell me why I shouldn't hang with Mattie because I am dying to hear this."

"You shouldn't be hanging with those types of people."

"Oh, dear Christian, who am I allowed to hang out with then because I thought the bible says to love all and judge not?"

"You are not supposed to walk with ungodly people Lynn. And I am not judging her, I am being honest." I yell.

"Well since we are being honest, you should be concerned about Mattie."

"What do you mean?"

"I'm just saying." She answers before walking into the closet, taking off her dress.

"You didn't have on any underwear?" I ask standing in the door.

"Nope."

"Lynn Nicole Watson, did you cheat on me?"

"Nope." She says walking pass me into the bathroom. "Not unless almost counts."

Lynn

The next morning, I roll over to Jerome sitting on the couch in our bedroom staring at me.

I don't bother to even say anything. I throw the covers back and get up.

"Where are you going?" He asks.

I walk into the bathroom.

"Lynn, I asked you a question. You cannot say you almost cheated and expect us not to talk about it?"

I close the door and turn on the shower.

I take my time washing my hair, pulling it up into a bun and then washing my body. When I am done, I get out and oil down while I am still wet. I brush my teeth and wash my face before opening the door.

Wrapping a towel around me, I open the door and suddenly the lights go out and the sound of Tank's, *'When We'* begins to play through the Bluetooth.

My mouth falls open as I step farther into the room to see the curtains pulled shut and the candles from last night relit. Jerome is standing beside the bed, stark naked with a bow on his penis.

I quickly recover from my shock and put my mad face back on. "Jerome, what are you doing? You look foolish."

I try to move him but he grabs my arm.

"Lynn Nicole Watson, I was the biggest fool on last night. You'd gone through the trouble, on your birthday, for me and I acted like a complete idiot. Please forgive me."

"It's fine Jerome. I'm over it."

He walks behind me and kisses me on my shoulder.

"Instead of me giving you forty kisses in private places, I allowed you to leave. Please forgive me."

He kisses me in the middle of my back.

"Instead of making you scream my name, the right way, I had you screaming in anger. Please forgive me."

This time when he kissed me on the small of my back, I moan.

He stands up behind me, allowing me to feel his erection on my butt before whispering in my ear. "I am so sorry for ruining your birthday baby. Please forgive me."

I open my mouth but no words come out.

He walks in front of me, pulling me to him as he sits on the bed.

"Do you forgive me Lynn?"

"I don't know yet, what else you got?" I ask, smiling.

"Oh, I'm only getting started." He replies, snatching me by the arm onto the bed causing me to giggle.

He takes his time, paying special attention to each of my breast. He moves down to my stomach then my navel, stopping at my bikini line using his tongue to trace the scar from the two caesarean surgeries.

I moan my pleasure of him.

When he raises up, I open my eyes to see what he's doing.

"I found your friend." He says holding up my bullet.

"Oh." I say shockingly. "Well, you said you weren't into toys so--"

"So, let's see what he does that I can't."

He turns it on and presses it against me. I close my eyes and my mouth makes sounds, I don't think Jerome has ever heard.

"Hmm, I like the sound of that." He smiles. "I wonder what sound you'll make if I turn it on full speed?"

He increases the speed and my hand instinctively goes there as the orgasm begins to build. I spread my legs a little wider, causing him to sit back a little further.

"Oh God!" I cry out.

When my orgasm is over, I open my eyes to see Jerome smiling,

"You've definitely been holding out on me. What else you got?" He asks.

"Find my other toys and you'll see." I challenge.

*****

A few hours later, we wake because our stomachs were growling.

"Happy belated birthday Mrs. Watson."

"Thank you Mr. Watson." I respond, kissing him on the lips. I can feel him starting to 'wake' up. "No, you don't. Babe, we've been at it all morning."

"Then I suggest you get up and put some clothes on or we will never leave this bed."

"Say no more." I say getting ready to move but he stops me.

"Babe did something happen between you and Mattie last night."

"Jerome don't kill the mood."

"I'm not trying too but I am so sorry for pushing you out of this house for what you needed."

"Babe, here's the thing." I say sitting up. "We've been in this thang since we were seventeen. We grew up together, we learned our bodies together and you've been the only person I've ever been with. I don't want anybody but you however, you have to be willing to give me what I need and when you stop, what else am I supposed to do?"

"Would you cheat on me?"

"Yes." I pause. "But I'd tell you first. Wasn't that our promise?"

He looks at me.

"Before today, it had been six months since we had sex. SIX months Jerome. Do you know how horny I was? After a few drinks last night, Mattie almost got your stuff but thank God I had enough strength to stop myself." I tell him. "But what would have happened had I not."

"I don't know how to respond to that." He says.

"Me neither which makes me wonder, if you aren't having sex with me, what are you doing?"

"You think I'm cheating?" He asks me.

"Are you?"

"You would really ask me that?"

"It's just a question Jerome but don't respond, not yet because I want your honesty. Instead, do me a favor."

"I'm listening."

"Talk to one or a few of the men you fellowship with, down at the church and see how often they have sex with their wife and let's revisit this conversation. No arguing, just an open and honest conversation about the marriage bed. Deal?"

"I guess."

I kiss him. "I'm going to the gym."

"Hey, dinner and a movie later?"

"I'd like that."

Jerome

I walk into the conference room and everybody stops talking.

"What's going on? Did I miss something?" I ask.

"Have a seat Deacon Watson." Pastor Carrington says before calling the meeting to order.

After prayer, the secretary reads the minutes from last month's meeting and we discuss new business. When there are no more questions, everybody looks at Pastor Carrington.

"Now," Pastor Carrington says, "Deacon Watson, there is a matter we need to discuss."

"Okay, what is it?"

"This." Deacon Matthews states, turning his phone towards me.

My eyes buck at the picture of my wife dancing with Mattie and some more women.

"Keep scrolling because there are more." He says.

"I've seen enough." I tell him sliding his phone back.

"Did you know about this?" Pastor inquires.

"No, well yes. I mean Lynn told me she'd seen Mattie while she was out last night, but I didn't know she was at a club. Who took these and where did you get them?"

"That doesn't matter but I have to ask, are you okay with your wife hanging out at clubs, dressed like this and with her?" Deacon Matthews asks pointing to the phone.

"Of course not but my wife is grown and I cannot control where she goes and who she sees. Furthermore, it was her fortieth birthday."

"And that gives her the right to act like this? Are you the head of your house or is she?" Matthews bluntly questions. "Because no wife of mine would ever act like this."

"Wait just one minute!" I say standing up. "You will not question the authority of my house neither will you put your mouth on my wife when I don't speak on you and yours."

"Hold on gentleman." Pastor Carrington says. "Let's not take this to a place it doesn't belong."

I take my seat.

"Deacon Watson, we are not here to judge how you run your house neither are we trying to upset you. However, this matter was bought before us and we have a duty to speak to you about it." Pastor Carrington says.

"If that were the case, this would have been handled differently instead of bombarding me in this setting. Shouldn't I be offered respect as a member of this brotherhood and church?"

"You should."

"I apologize for overstepping." Deacon Matthews says. "I shouldn't have handled this situation like this."

"No, you shouldn't have because this is not a matter for a deacon board meeting. What you should have done is come to me as a brother and friend."

"You are absolutely right Deacon Watson." Pastor Carrington says. "Let me apologize on behalf of all of us."

"Thank you for your apology." I tell him. "And thank you for bringing this to my attention however I will not tell my wife who she can and cannot hang out with neither will I tell her how to dress. Lynn is a grown woman who has values and respect for herself, her family and her church and I do not believe she will do anything to embarrass any of us."

"Very well." Deacon Jones says. "Is there anything else?"

Everyone shakes their head no. Pastor Carrington prays and then dismisses the meeting.

"Deacon Watson, can I talk to you in my office for a moment?"

"Sure."

I follow him across the hall, closing the door while he sits behind his desk.

"Jerome, you have to know we didn't mean to insinuate anything about your house, don't you?"

"No, I don't because of the way this was handled. Bringing this before the deacon board was out of line." I respond taking a seat in the chair.

"You are correct and it will not happen again. Now, is there something going on with you and Lynn?"

"Pastor Carrington, you have known Lynn and I for over ten years and you know she rarely goes out. She only did, last night because she was upset with me. Things have been rocky lately and on top of that I forgot her birthday."

"Man, what were you thinking? You never forget birthdays and anniversaries."

"I know but I have so much going on with hiring the new youth pastor, finishing next year's budget for the church along with this huge project I have at work that needs a foreman I can trust; I've been busy."

"I get that but your family should always be your first ministry and home should come before anything, especially this church. Look Jerome, the last thing you want is for your wife to feel unappreciated. I get that you are committed to your job and role on the deacon board but none of these Negroes will be able to keep you warm if your wife chooses divorce."

"You're right but I don't know what to do. I messed up."

"Man, forgetting her birthday isn't the end of the world."

"I've been having an affair." I blurt.

Pastor Carrington's mouth open. "I, wow, I wasn't expecting that. Does Lynn know?" He asks.

"No."

"You have to tell her."

"I don't know how. Pastor, I cannot lose my wife."

He shakes his head. "What made you cheat?"

"Being stupid but you want to hear something crazy? Lynn almost cheated last night and she admitted it to me this morning. I sat there like a complete idiot while my wife confessed her indiscretions and I couldn't have blamed her if she did because before this morning, I hadn't touched her in over six months yet she's still faithful to me."

"Jerome, I cannot tell you how to handle the situation but I will tell you this, you need to tell her before she finds out some other way. Also, stop neglecting your wife because while you're not doing what she needs, you leave her open to the schemes of the enemy and if there is no sex happening in the marriage bed, it is bound to happen outside of it?"

I drop my head.

"It hurts when the shoe is on the other foot because even if your wife didn't cheat, the thought along doesn't feel good, does it?"

I shake my head no.

"Your marriage can be restored son but you have to know that the bible says in Hebrews 13:4, ""Let marriage be held in honor among all, and let the marriage bed be undefiled, for God will judge the sexually immoral and adulterous."

"I know and the judging is what I'm afraid of."

"You have to be able to take the consequences of your actions. Let's pray before you leave." He says.

I stand up and he walks over and grabs one hand and places the other on my shoulder.

"Dear God, thank you for the blood of your son Jesus for it was His blood that gave us repentance for our sins. Forgive us God, for the sins we have committed knowingly or unknowingly. And God, as we petition your throne today, I ask a special prayer for Jerome. You know his deeds and your word says, if we repent with our mouth you will forgive us. Grant him wisdom to do what he knows is right and to repair his marriage. Strengthen him to resist temptation and to see evil before it shows up. Guide him now God. Amen."

"Amen. Thank you pastor."

"No problem. Give Lynn my love and I'll be here for the both of you if you need it."

Walking out, my phone vibrates with a text from an unsaved number.

UNSAVED NUMBER: I need to see you.

ME: Who is this?

UNSAVED NUMBER: You know who it is. I need to see you.

ME: Why are you texting my phone and not through the app? You know the rules.

UNSAVED NUMBER: Rules are meant to be broken. Right, daddy?

ME: Not today but I agree, we need to talk … Monday.

UNSAVED NUMBER: Whatever!

Lynn

Walking to the locker room, someone bumps into me.

"Hey, it's you. My special VIP from last night."

I look up at the fine specimen of a man from the club.

"And you're the one who helped to make my birthday special. I didn't get the chance to tell you thank you, by the way. Thank you, I'm Lynn." I say extending my hand.

"You're welcome and it is nice to officially meet you Lynn, I'm Mateo." He says. "Are you a member here?"

"I am. You?" I inquire.

"I am. Do you mind if I ask you a question?"

"Sure."

"Are you married?"

"Yes." I say flashing my ring.

"Happily?"

"That depends on the day." I laugh.

"Well, I can keep a secret if you can." He says walking close to me.

"I'm flattered Mateo but my answer is no."

He sticks out his lip. "Well, if you're ever in need of a real man, look me up."

I smile as I walk into the locker room, taking my time to grab my things, in case he is still in the hall. I peek out the door and when I don't see him, I make a beeline for my car.

Getting inside, I start it and pull off. I press the Bluetooth to dial Jerome's number but he doesn't answer. I wait a minute and call him again but still no answer so I make a stop at the juice bar.

I get ready to open the door when I hear Jerome's voice.

I let the door close and make the turn to the patio where I see him sitting at a table, laughing.

I walk over.

"What's so funny?" I ask.

"Babe," he says pushing the chair back to stand up. "What are you doing here?"

"It's a juice bar Jerome but the question is, what are you doing here?"

"I was—this is Sydney, she is the new Youth Pastor at High Point. Sydney, this is my wife Lynn."

"It's nice to finally meet you Sydney. I feel like I know you with all the meetings and paperwork Jerome has been dealing with during this hiring process."

"It has been a process." She laughs. "And he's right, when he said we could be sisters."

"I agree. I love your hair. Let me know if you need some natural hair products, since you're new to the climate here in Memphis."

"I definitely will but why don't you join us." She says moving her purse from the chair. "We're just talking about church stuff."

"No thanks, I'm all sweaty. I just stopped to get a smoothie but I'll let you all finish your conversation. Are we still on for dinner and a movie?" I ask Jerome.

"Of course. I'll meet you at the house in thirty."

"Make it an hour." I reply. "Sydney, again, it was nice to finally meet you. I will see you on tomorrow and I look forward to hearing you at Assembly."

Jerome kisses me goodbye before I go inside, order my smoothie and head home.

*****

The next morning, I walk into High Point Christian Assembly. Jerome always leaves ahead of me because he goes to Sunday school and well, I don't.

"Good morning," I practically sing to Mildred, a greeter but she turns away from me. I walk over to where she is. "Um, Mildred, is there a problem?"

"What do you mean dear?" She asks.

"I spoke to you and you acted like you didn't hear me."

"I'm sorry, I didn't hear you. Good morning Lynn."

"You did but it's cool. I hope you have a great rest of your day."

I walk inside the sanctuary and Mattie grabs my arm.

"Hey girl." She says.

"Hey."

"What's wrong? This isn't about Friday is it?" She asks whispering.

"Huh? Oh no, I spoke to Mildred and she acted like she didn't hear me."

"Oh, it's probably because of the pictures." She says releasing my arm.

"Pictures?"

"Your husband didn't tell you?"

I guess my face answered her.

"Child, somebody took pictures of us dancing at The Underground, Friday night and sent them to a few of the deacons. I'm shocked Jerome didn't tell you seeing they questioned his ability to be the head of his house? You know you aren't supposed to hang around with me."

"Girl screw them." I state, bluntly.

"I would if I wasn't gay but give me the wives any day of the week and twice on Sunday."

We both laugh loud enough for people to look at us.

"How do you get all the gossip?" I ask her.

"Baby, this isn't gossip, its gospel. Shoot, you'll be surprised the spouses I have access too." She laughs. "And Mrs. Thang, you and the husband must have made up, I see." She says pointing to my neck.

"I don't know what you are talking about."

"Then how did you get that hickey on your neck?"

I giggle. "Girl, I burned myself with the curlers."

"What curlers when your hair has been natural since you came out your momma's wah-hoo?"

Before I can respond to her foolishness, the worshipper leader stands to start service.

"We will talk." I say laughing before walking off.

The Marriage Bed

Worship Service

"How many of you know we serve a wonder working God?" Tamara says to the congregation. "This song is simple, sing it with me."

"Way maker, miracle worker, promise keeper, light in the darkness; my God that is who you are. Way maker, miracle worker, promise keeper, light in the darkness; my God that is who you are. "

"If you believe God is a way maker and miracle worker, stand to your feet and join us."

"Way maker, miracle worker, promise keeper, light in the darkness; my God that is who you are.

After a few selections, devotion, welcome, announcements and offering; Asst. Pastor Rogers calls for altar call. I walk down and Jerome holds out his hand, for me to take as the music changes to Thank You Lord.

"Shall we bow for a word of prayer? Heavenly Father, we come petitioning your throne this morning, first to tell you thank you. Thank you for allowing our eyes to open and see a new day. Thank you God, for the activities of our limbs and being in our right mind and thank you for reasonable portion of health and strength. Now God, I ask you to move around this altar because too many of your people are bound, free them.

There are too many of your people sick, heal them. God, listen to their hearts and grant what they ask of you, if it is in your will. Destroy the chains of oppression and depression, bind yokes that seek to destroy marriages, release supernatural prosperity and open blinded eyes and ears that have been shut off to hearing your word. God, we need you.

Not only in this house but every house that stands open in your name. Bless today, heal today, deliver today, set free today and restore. For the tithes and offerings that have been raised, increase them and then God, give back to all those who have given to you. We thank you God and we will forever give your name glory. These things we ask. Amen. It's fellowship time." He says. "Stir around and hug your neighbors and welcome any visitor."

"Erica?"

"Lynn, hey."

"Is this your first time coming to High Point?" I ask giving her a hug.

"Yea, church is really not my thing but I spent the night with Mattie and she has been begging me to come so I thought today was as good as any to get it over with."

I laugh. "Well welcome and I hope you will enjoy the service. Who knows, one of these days you might join."

"Wait, is the man you hugged your husband?" Erica asks pointing to Jerome.

"Yes, do you know him?"

"He looks familiar but maybe not. You know they say, we all have a twin somewhere. Anyway, I'll let you get back to worship. It was good seeing you."

"Yea, you too." I reply looking from him to her.

After fellowship and a selection by the choir, Pastor Carrington walks to the podium.

"Good morning High Point. Did anybody come to worship with a praise on your lips? Did anybody come to tell God thank you for letting you see a new day? Did anybody come yearning for a word from God? Don't fool me now, is anybody here thankful to serve a forgiving God?"

He waits until the crowd quiets down.

"I know you all have been wondering about our youth program, but I am happy to announce the newest member of our ministry team, Pastor Sydney Gable."

She stands as the congregation claps.

"And a huge thanks goes out to our deacon board, especially Deacon Jerome Watson for handling all of the necessary meetings and phone calls needed for her to come onboard. Lynn, I hope we didn't take up too much of Jerome's time."

When everyone looks at me, I nod and smiles.

"Now High Point, turn with me in your bibles to a familiar passage, John chapter five, verses two through four."

We all stand.

"Now there is in Jerusalem by the sheep gate a pool, which is called in Hebrew Bethesda, having five porticoes. In these lay a multitude of those who were sick, blind, lame, and withered, waiting for the moving of the waters; for an angel of the Lord went down at certain seasons into the pool and stirred up the water; whoever then first, after the stirring up of the water, stepped in was made well from whatever disease with which he was afflicted. The word of God for the people of God. Take your seats."

"This morning, if I had to pen a particular tag line to this passage, it would be, it's not your season yet. Look at your neighbor and tell them, It's not your season yet."

My thoughts are consumed with Erica asking about Jerome. I look at him and he's into the service. I try to shake it off as I listen to the sermon.

"Come here lame man by the pool of Bethesda. Here is what we know about him. He was a man who was ill for 38 years. That's it. We don't know what his infirmity was but we do know it was to the point, he could hardly walk. We don't know if he lived by the pool or if someone dropped him off, daily but we know he was there. And for however long he tried, he couldn't get well. Bible says, at certain seasons, the angel of the Lord would come down and move the water and whoever was the first to get in, got healed.

Yet, this man didn't stop coming. Although the season would come for the angel to show up, it wasn't his season to be healed. But he kept coming. The angel kept coming to trouble the water and he still wasn't healed but he kept coming. We don't know how many trips he'd made to the pool or how many years he'd had to wait but he's been lame for 38 years and still coming. It wasn't his season yet. Then along comes

Jesus, on His way to the cross that happens to have Him stop by the pool of Bethesda."

"How many of you know, when Jesus shows up things happen?"

"Amen Pastor!"

"Speak sir!"

"I need somebody to know, your season is coming but you need to be patient. You may be lying on your bed of affliction, dealing with some denials and suffering in sickness and but your season is coming. Yes, I know every time you look around others are being blessed and not you. You feel like this man, telling Jesus; every time the water is troubled someone beats me to my deliverance.

You are looking around and see the crowd is starting to thin out but you're still there. All the folks before you have gotten their blessing and gone and you're still waiting, trying to figure out, when will it be my time? Glancing at your watch and Jesus still hasn't come. Peeking through the blinds and morning still hasn't shown up. Beloved, it is not your season yet.

I have come to know that God will put you in a painful place, intentionally and allow you to hurt. God will deliberately place you around folk who talk about you, all day long and you'll know it. God is going to assign you some stuff to do, you know don't make sense to your natural and it will benefit everybody but you. Why? Because your season has not yet come."

The spirit in the church rises as Pastor closes his sermon. I look at Jerome and our eyes connect. I smile and he smiles back.

Jerome

I gaze over at Lynn and when our eyes connect, we both smile. I feel my phone vibrate. I pull it out to see a text from an unknown number.

UNKNOWN: I need to see you.

ME: You will, tomorrow.

UNKNOWN: NO! Today, it's important.

ME: I don't care how important it is, weekends are off limits.

UNKNOWN: Not if I tell.

ME: I am sick of you and these threats.

UNKNOWN: It's not a threat. Maybe I'll wait for church to be over and tell your wife how good her husband tastes. Now, let's try this again. I need to see you Jerome.

ME: Fine!

UNKNOWN: I knew you'd see it my way. Love you. ❤

When I look up, Lynn is in the midst of worship and my heart drops into the pit of my stomach.

Once church is over, I grab my bible and turn to see Erica.

"You're married?" She whispers.

I look back but I don't see Lynn.

"Erica, what are you doing here?"

"My friend invited me but don't change the subject. ARE.YOU.MARRIED?"

"Yes, but I can't do this right now." I say at a whisper before raising my voice. "It was great to have you with us today. I hope you enjoyed worship and will come again." I shake her hand and walk off.

I was headed for the door until I see Deacon Matthews walk over to Lynn who is talking to a few members.

"Well, if it isn't Ms. Shake Your Thang." I hear him say.

"What did you call me?" Lynn asks.

"Raymond, you need to back up." I tell him.

"I was only joking. Calm down."

"Don't joke with me, joke with your momma." Lynn says before walking off.

When we get in the car and get our seatbelts on, we both speak at the same time.

"Go ahead." I state, starting the car and pulling off.

"Why didn't you tell me about the pictures sent to the deacon board?"

"It slipped my mind."

"What about the part where they questioned your ability to run your household." She asks.

"How do you know about that?"

"Jerome, what right do they have to say anything about our house? I am willing to bet it was old Deacon Matthews with his meddling self. He is always up in other people's business when he needs to worry about his undercover wife. Baby, they better be glad it was you they said that crap too because I would have been thrown out of High Point Assembly."

"Are you done?" I ask once she finishes her tirade.

"No! As a matter of fact, I'm pissed like you should be."

"I told you I have it taken care of." I tell her. "But you shouldn't have said what you said."

"You better be glad that is all I said. Calling me, sweet thang. How dare him."

"Regardless of what he said Lynn, you need to remain respectful. This is our place of worship and he is the head of the deacon board."

"And? He's also just a man Jerome, not God. He puts his pants on the same way we do. That's the problem, y'all give him too much power and he thinks he can get away with saying and doing stuff like this. Me, I don't care who he is, he doesn't have the right to say anything he wants and get away with it."

"You still need to respect him."

"I give respect when it's given." She says.

"Well this never would have happened had you had your ass at home!" I yell.

"Wait, are you seriously blaming me for this?"

"You had to know there would be backlash for being out with Mattie and her friends?"

"Is this 1918 or 2018 because I could have sworn I turned 40 and not 16."

"Then you need to act like it because no decent woman should have been out that time of hour and especially with the likes of Mattie. Everybody knows she's gay yet you're out booty dancing with her for the world to see. You should be ashamed of yourself."

"I am."

"Good." I sigh before pulling into the gas station. When I put the car in gear, I take my seatbelt off and open the door then I pause. "I don't want you texting or interacting with Mattie or her friends again."

"Is there anything else daddy?" She mocks in a childish voice.

"Take it how you want Lynn but you have no business hanging with them."

She grabs my arm to stop me from getting out.

"You know Jerome, I am ashamed. Ashamed that my husband has been brained washed by a group of men who probably haven't touched their wives in years but will proposition choir members. I am ashamed you actually think you can tell me who I can and cannot talk too. And I am even more ashamed of who you have allowed yourself to become in the name of Christianity." She counters before unfastening her seatbelt.

"Where are you going?"

"To get you a snicker because you're acting like a bit—"

"Lynn!"

Lynn

I walk into the gas station and right into the chest of somebody.

"Lynn?"

"Mateo?" I say looking at him then back to see Jerome pumping gas.

"Are you okay?" He asks.

"Yea, I'm good. What about you?" I ask stepping farther inside.

"Better now that I've laid eyes on you again." He smiles, stepping closer to me.

When he gets ready to put his arms around me, I move back. "What are you doing?"

"I was only going to give you a hug."

"Oh, that's not necessary." I state.

"Are you sure you're okay? Did something happen?"

"What do you mean?"

"The way you got out the car. Did the man upset you?"

"That man is my husband."

"He must not be good at it because if you were mine--"

"I'm sorry but I am not yours. As a matter of fact, I find it odd that I've bumped into you twice within the last two days."

"Maybe it's fate." He says.

"And maybe it's not. Either way it's creepy. Excuse me."

I turn to go leave but he grabs my arm.

"Lynn, why are you fighting this? You seemed interested when I was buying your drinks."

I turn back to him and snatch my arm away.

"Are you serious?"

"Very?" He smiles.

"If I can recall, Mateo, you offered to buy my drinks, I didn't request. However, let me repay you so you can leave me the hell alone." I reach into my wallet and pull out a ten-dollar bill. "Here, this should cover the *one* mojito you gave me. It wasn't good anyway."

"Lynn are you okay?" Jerome asks from behind me.

I turn around but Mateo steps in front of me.

"No, she's not but don't worry, I'll take care of her." Mateo answers.

"Will you please move!" I say.

Mateo doesn't move. He turns back to me. "Estas bien mi amor?"

"Look dude, we don't know what you said and neither do we care. It would be best, for the both of us, if you go on." Jerome says.

"Is that what you want mi pronto ser?"

"Mi pronto ser?" I repeat, confused.

"My soon to be." Mateo says rubbing my face. I slap his hand away.

"Dude, the only thing, soon to be, is your ass being kicked if you don't take your hand off my wife."

Mateo laughs.

"Mateo, I don't know what your problem is but please leave me alone. If I see you following me again, I will call the police."

He blows me a kiss before walking off.

"Who was that?" Jerome asks.

"Let's just go."

We ride in silence for a few minutes.

"Who was that?" Jerome asks breaking through the thick air in the car.

"The owner of the club I went to the other night."

"Do you know him?"

"I just told you, I met him at the club the other night."

"He seemed overly concerned about you."

"I know and it's creepy." I state.

"Are you having an affair?"

I laugh. He doesn't.

"Are you serious?"

"Yes, this dude was very interested in you and I just fail to believe you just met him."

"You're joking, right? Please tell me you're joking."

"I'm only stating the obvious Lynn."

"Jerome, what is going on? Why are we arguing after the day we had yesterday?" I ask sighing.

"This isn't arguing but I can't help but wonder why you're so interested in sex toys and--"

"You didn't seem to have an issue with them yesterday though." I say.

"I did that for you." He blurts. "Did he turn you on to them?"

"Did who turn me on to what?"

"Your little Spanish boyfriend?" Jerome says trying to mimic Mateo's voice. "Have you used toys with him?"

"Yes Jerome. We use them every second Tuesday, when we meet up for our bi-weekly sex sessions once you and the children are gone."

"For all I know you could have." He replies.

"You think that much or should I say that less of me?" I ask looking at him. "You actually believe I would cheat on you?"

"Right now I don't know what to think because you are the one who is acting differently." He says. "You buy lingerie, sex toys, you go out to clubs and hang with lesbians. To be honest, I don't know who you are anymore."

"Where is all of this coming from? For the last six months, all I have talked about is celebrating my fortieth birthday WITH YOU. I told you what I wanted which was a weekend at home with you, doing the kinds of things we used to do. Things to spice up our marriage bed. Now suddenly, it's a problem. Why?"

I don't say anything.

"Why Jerome? Why is it I can trust you but you can't trust me? Why is it, you can have lunch with women and I never bat an eye but you see me, in an uncomfortable position and instead of coming to my rescue, you accuse me of cheating. Why?"

Jerome

"Answer me!" Lynn screams.

"I'm only trying to figure out where this change is coming from."

"Oh okay, that's it. It has nothing to do with the fact you haven't touched your wife, sexually, in six months."

"No, I told you."

"No Jerome, you haven't told me anything. All you've done is accused me."

"What do you want from me Lynn?" I ask.

"Honesty."

I don't say anything.

"Take me home Jerome."

"I'm sorry." I state.

"What are you sorry for?"

"For everything."

"What does that mean? Why are you speaking in code? What are you sorry for? JUST BE HONEST!!"

!!CAR HORN BLARES!!

I hit on brakes to keep from hitting the car in front of me.

After a few seconds, I begin to drive again.

"Please take me home." Lynn says.

"Aren't we picking the kids up for dinner?"

"No."

We continue the drive home in silence. I pull into the garage, put the car in park and turn it off. Lynn unfastens her seat belt and turns to me.

"I'm going to my parent's house for a little while."

"Babe don't leave like this because you're angry." I tell her.

"I'm not angry Jerome but I am confused."

"Confused about what?"

"I am confused about what transpired during the time you left for church until the time church was over that put you into the mood you're currently in.

And don't act like it was dude at the gas station because you were acting stank before that. What happened?"

I open my mouth to say something but she holds up her hand.

"You know what, never mind. Here's what is about to happen. I'm going to get out of your car then I'm going to my parents where I will stay for a little while. Once I'm done, I'm coming home. That should give you, um, a good one to three hours."

"One to three hours to do what?"

"Figure out a way to tell your wife the truth."

I watch as Lynn gets out of my car and into hers. When she backs out the driveway, I let the garage down and go in the house.

Going over to the wet bar, I make a Hennessy and Coke before walking to the bedroom. I sit my drink on the nightstand, along with my phone and keys then remove my pants, tie and shirt throwing them across the bed. Once I am down to only my boxers and t-shirt, I sit on the side of the bed with my phone and open the messenger app.

ME: Are you there?

A few seconds later, a response.

BOO: Yes, are you on the way?

ME: No, I'm not coming. Look, I can't do this anymore.

BOO: I figured as much. It's cool.

ME: You are getting too attached and carried away with your threats. I cannot allow you to ruin all that I have worked hard for.

BOO: You can't allow me to ruin it? You took vows, not me.

ME: I know and I am sorry for ever getting involved with you.

BOO: Oh, you might not be now but you will be.

ME: What is that supposed to mean?

No response.

ME: Hello?

I go to grab my drink and waste some on my hand.

Shaking the liquid off, I head into the bathroom. I sit the phone on the sink and turn on the water to wash my hands when I hear the chirp of the alarm.

"Lynn?"

I turn off the water.

Another sound.

I walk out of the bedroom and down the hall.

"Lynn are you here?"

When I turn the corner … "What are you doing in my house?"

"Finishing our conversation. Drink?"

"No and you need to leave."

"Either have a drink or I'll sit here until the wife and children get home. You think you can explain my being here then."

I laugh. "I am not scared of your threats anymore and I am tired of doing this. You can stay here until Jesus returns because my wife will never believe anything you have to say."

"No but she might believe what I have to show her."

She punches something on her phone and a video begins to play of me and her having sex.

"You were saying?" She asks.

Lynn

"Hey mom, what are you doing here? I thought we were staying until tomorrow?" Mallory, our youngest asks when I walk into my parent's house.

"I missed you guys. Is that okay?"

"Sure, but where's dad?"

"He had some work to do."

"He's going to miss Sunday dinner?" She pouts.

"Yea but he'll make it up to you. Where is everybody?"

"My brother and sister are upstairs. Grandpa is taking a nap and grandma is in her office."

"Well, if you all want to come home with me tonight, get your things together while I talk to momma." I tell her. Walking to my mom's office, I tap on the door.

"Come in."

I push the door open and see her getting off the floor.

"Did I interrupt your prayer time?"

"No, I was finished. Come in. I thought you weren't coming until tomorrow."

I close the door and walk over to give her a hug.

"What's wrong?" She asks.

"I think Jerome is having an affair." I say bursting into tears.

"Aw hell, girl stop crying." She says handing me the box of Kleenex from the desk and we both sit on the couch.

"I don't know what else to do."

"Do you have proof?"

I shake my head no.

"Have you asked him?"

I shake my head yes.

"And?"

"He denied it." I say.

"Then get proof or are you afraid it might be true."

"I'm scared. If Jerome is having an affair, our entire life will change."

"And?"

"Ma, we've been together since I was seventeen." I answer wiping my face.

"I know but what does that have to do with anything? It does not matter if you two were together since you were six, things happen that are not in our control. What you can control is how you deal with it but first, you need to find out if there is anything going on. No need in getting worked up over suspicion."

"I know he's cheating, I can feel it."

"Baby, I love you but you have got to get out of your feelings when it comes to this kind of thing. Yes, you love your husband but being emotional will throw you off your game. Woman up because you've put too many years into this man just to hand him over to somebody else."

"Ma, I am not in the business of keeping a man who does not want to be kept."

"Who said anything about keeping him? Child, if he wants to go, let him but ensure he leaves the bank account intact. Have you two stopped having sex yet?"

I look at her with a shocked face. "How--"

"You are not the first person to go through this. How long has it been?"

"Before yesterday, six months."

"And you're just now saying something?"

"I was giving him the benefit of the doubt because he has been so busy."

"Baby, there isn't a man alive who is too busy for sex. What are you going to do?"

"I don't know. If it were just me, I'd leave him but what about the children?" I ask.

"What about them?"

"A divorce will devastate them."

"Those children are older and capable of understanding but stop getting ahead of yourself. You first must know if your husband is, in fact, cheating. If he is, then the two of you need to decide what's next. Look Lynn, I am all for marriage but not at the expense of your sanity. If your marriage can be restored, do it but don't be a fool and please don't hold on to a piece of a man for the sake of having a husband because you never have to chase what belongs to you."

"What do I do?"

"You pray and ask God to uncover what is hidden but only if you are indeed ready to deal with it. Then you get off your butt and be the wife and mother you've always been. Don't allow this, whatever it is, to take you out of character. Stay true to Lynn. While you do this, be careful of temptations."

"What do you mean?"

"Lynn, you're seeking the attention of your husband for something you've been missing. The enemy will use what you're longing for to tempt you, but you've got to keep your eyes open and your hormones in check because a man or a woman, showing you're the attention you're lacking, can be detrimental to you. Don't fall for it. I don't care how good he or she looks and smells or even how he or she promises to make you feel; walk away."

I put my head down.

"Oh my God, please tell me you haven't cheated." She says.

"Of course not mother!"

"Whew." She exclaims.

"But I want too. I want too badly."

"Girl, we need your daddy's prayers for this."

Jerome

I rush towards her but she holds up a gun. I stop and put up my hands.

"Why are you doing this?"

"Why am I doing this? Why did you do this? You came after me?" She asks pointing the gun back and forth between us.

"I didn't. You pursued me with the texts and videos. You were the one who showed up at my office."

"Yea but you didn't stop yourself from shoving your penis down my throat either!" She yells.

"I know and I'm sorry. I didn't mean for things to go this far."

"But they have and a year later, things have definitely gone far."

"Look, I should have never crossed the line with you and I'm sorry, but I can't continue to do this."

"You can't continue? I've put my life on hold for you and now you shouldn't have crossed the line? Baby you should have thought about that before you sent nude pictures holding your penis in your hands. You crossed the line when you had my legs spread across your desk at Watson Construction and your lips on my lips down below. You crossed the line when you told me you loved me. You crossed the line when you impregnated me with your seed then paid for the abortion. You crossed the line when we made plans to be together. And you definitely crossed the line when we discussed killing your wife. So, shall we try this again? Drink?"

"Look, I'm sorry but I can't do this anymore. You need to leave."

"Okay."

"Good." I say letting out the breath it feels like I've been holding. "I never meant to hurt you. You must know that. I am sorry, but this is for the best."

"Oh, did you think my okay was in agreement with you? Oh no boo, that okay means I was tired of hearing you whining. However, what's about to happen is, you're going to make love to me or I will kill you."

"Please don't do this. Think about my children."

"You should have thought about your children before you messed up my life because they don't mean anything to me. You made me kill mine, remember."

"Please baby."

"Please baby." She mimics. "Choose."

"I said I was sorry. What more do you want?"

"Everything you promised me but for the moment, I'll take your penis so you can give me what I want or your family can view your body in three to five days. Your choice but make it quick because my drink is getting warm."

I pace around the kitchen, for a few seconds, before walking over and grabbing the drink.

"Look, I will have sex with you but don't do it like this, please. Not here."

"It's not like we haven't done it here before. You remember when your wife and kids went out of town and we spent the entire weekend, here, in bed?"

"Shut up!" I scream.

"Boo, I'm only holding you accountable for the promises you made. You told me I was the one you wanted to be with. You told me I was the one who had your heart and the only reason you haven't left is the kids. Remember?"

"I know what I said."

"Then stand by your words, NEGRO!"

I jump when she points the gun at me.

"I'm sorry. Woosah." She says. "Look, you ought to be glad I am not asking you to divorce your wife. Hell, if you want, she can join us because I've been wanting to taste her anyway. Man, I bet she gets wet and--"

"Leave my wife out of this!"

She laughs. "Are you scared she may get what she's been missing."

"I'm not about to tell you again. After today, it's over. Do you hear me? Don't come here again." I shout before I down the drink in one swallow.

"Yo hago las reglas!" She yells. "Did you hear me? I make the rules."

"NO! I mean it. After today it's --" I stumble back.

I feel myself being led down the hall. Once inside the room, she pushes me onto the bed.

I feel my lips moving but nothing is coming out.

"What did you say papi? I can't hear you." She says over me.

I try to move my arm but I can't.

"Shh, I promise I'll be gentle."

Lynn

After spending more time than I'd planned, at my parents, the kids and I finally make it home. It's after nine and Jerome's car is in the garage but the house is dark.

"Jerome," I call out when I open the door. "Jerome?"

The alarm is set to stay so I know he's here.

"He must be asleep." I tell the children.

"Do you want me to wake him and give him his food?" Nathaniel, our son, asks.

"No, put it in the microwave and he'll eat it when he gets up."

He shrugs before walking off.

The children disperse to their rooms and I go towards mine. I stop because the door is closed.

I twist the knob and its pitch black.

"Jerome."

I turn on the light and he is in the bed. I walk over, pull the covers back and he is naked and it's obvious he hasn't been alone.

"Jerome!" I say hitting him.

"Hmm," he mumbles.

"Jerome, wake your ass up!"

He mumbles again.

I close the door before walking into the bathroom to look around for something, anything. I stop when I see his phone on the sink. I pick it up and it's locked.

I press the home button.

Touch ID or Enter Passcode

Stepping back into the bedroom, I call his name again but he doesn't move so I take his thumb and unlock the phone. It comes up to a message app.

BOO: You can't allow me to ruin it? You took vows, not me.

ME: I know and I am sorry for ever getting involved with you.

BOO: Oh, you might not be now but you will be.

ME: What is that supposed to mean?

ME: Hello?

I sit on the side of the bed and begin to read through the messages on his phone. The more I scroll up, the more vulgar the messages gets. Tears are streaming down my face as I cannot believe some of the things he has said to her. And the pictures … oh my God.

"Wow." I say out loud realizing he has an account set up for her at Victoria's Secrets. "But you laughed when I wore lingerie. Oh ok."

I continue scrolling through the messages and to know *my* husband is talking like this to somebody else makes me sick at the stomach.

"When can I see what that mouth do?"

"I'll be at the office late tonight, waiting to spread you across my desk."

"You left your juices on my desk."

"Who's your daddy?"

I continue to scroll but then a message comes in.

BOO: I'm sorry for the way I handled things tonight. I got carried away. I never should have come to your house, again.

I contemplate whether to reply.

ME: Are you sorry for being in my bed or for screwing my husband?

BOO: Oh, is this wife? Our husband must still be asleep? Lol.

ME: Who are you?

BOO: Lynn, Lynn, quite contrary; how great thy bed feels. I know you're wondering who I am but wait, it's not time for US to tell. – Signed, HIS Mistress, Boo ♥

ME: Lol. There is nothing contrary about me but I'm glad you enjoyed my bed because you nor he will ever get the chance to feel it again. As for him, you can have him.

BOO: Aw, don't be like that. Bible says a marriage bed is undefiled.

ME: Isn't that something? A mistress who can quote scripture. I know you make Jesus so proud.

BOO: If He isn't, our husband is. Kiss him goodnight for me.

ME: You should have done that yourself because I can assure you, my lips will never touch another part of his body. As a matter of fact, you should have stayed until I got here to take him and his shit with you.

BOO: Nah, I want him to leave you on his own.

ME: Well, good luck with that sweetie.

BOO: I don't need luck when I have this creamy goodness between my thighs that keeps him cumming, oops, I mean coming back.

ME: Girl, if you say so. Wait up for him and I'll send him to you unless you're not as great as you think. Let us see, shall we?

I go back into the bathroom and empty the cup that has my makeup brushes in it and fill it with cold water. Returning to the room, I throw it on his face.

"Ahh--" he screams, looking around in a daze. "Lynn, what the hell?"

"Same question I have for you dear husband. Who is boo?"

When he sees his phone in my hand, he can't say anything.

"Um hello," I say snapping my fingers in his face. "Don't get quiet now. You have some explaining to do."

When he looks down and realizes he's naked, his head falls back on the pillow.

"Yea, you're screwed."

Jerome

I slowly get up and throw my legs over the side of the bed. "Lynn, what are you talking about? Ah, my head is throbbing,"

"Which head because it looks like both have been used tonight."

"What?" I ask her. "I don't know what you're talking about."

She laughs before walking over to the dresser, picking up a vase and throwing it. It barely misses my head. "Please don't treat me like I'm stupid Jerome! You know my throwing arm is good, which means I missed your head on purpose so let's try this again. Who in the hell is boo?"

"I don't know."

"Okay." She says as I watch her pull my phone from her back pocket and punching something.

"What are you doing with my phone?"

"Apparently talking to your mistress and the messages between the two of you are quite interesting. Let me read a few of them."

"Don't. Just give me my phone."

"No, they are really good." She sits in the chair. "Um, let's see. Oh, how about I read some of the ones from the day of my birthday. Good morning beautiful, I went to bed thinking about you. I wish I could have woken up to your warm lips wrapped around my--"

"Stop! Lynn, stop."

"No, they get better because you sent her a picture of your penis. In which she replies, damn papi, I can't wait to feel you on the back of my throat again. Too bad it's the wife's birthday. Don't give her my good stuff, either, she says. And you had me believing you forgot."

"I'm sorry." I tell her.

"Oh wait, here's another one. I wonder what you were thinking when I was deep throating you in the car while at your son's soccer practice."

"Lynn, please stop."

"No, wait because I need to read you the one she just sent." She says as tears fall. "Wifey girl, those satin sheets felt great against my naked skin. I'll have to get our husband to buy me the same ones. Oh, and tell Jerome, when he wakes up that I left something for him."

I drop my head in my hands.

"Lynn, I am so sorry."

"Who is she?"

I don't answer.

"WHO IS SHE JEROME?" She screams.

"Mom." Mallory's voice calls from the outside of the door.

She gets up and opens it. "What's wrong baby girl?"

"I don't feel good." Mallory says. "My chest hurts."

"Okay baby. Give me a minute and I'll be right there to give you a breathing treatment."

Mallory leaves and Lynn closes the door. I have my head in my hands when she turns back.

"HELLO!" Lynn yells, clapping her hands. "I'm going to ask you for the last time, who did you have in our bed?"

"Lynn, I don't know what you're talking about?" I say falling back onto the bed. "My head is killing me."

"You don't know what I'm talking about?" She repeats before walking over to the other side of bed, pulling back the covers.

"What are you doing? Stop because you're pissing me off!"

"Yea, I'm real scared of the man with two throbbing heads." She says. "Dude, unless you're living a double life where you cross dress in red lace thongs, you're lying."

"I promise I don't know what's going on." I reply never opening my eyes. "I think I was drugged."

"Then let me call 911."

I jump up.

"No, don't do that."

"It's mighty funny you can jump up then, Mr. I Think I Was Drugged."

"I don't know what happened Lynn. You've got to believe me."

"I do."

I let out a breath.

"I believe you as much as I believe in the Lochness Monster so get on up and pack your shit because you cannot stay here. By the time I get back from checking on our daughter, you need to be gone."

"Where am I supposed to go?"

She goes over and picks up my phone.

"Boo is expecting you."

She then throws the phone and it clips me on the side of the head.

I wait until she leaves before I pick up my phone. My head is hurting but not as bad as I pretended. I quickly open the app and see the messages.

"Mother--"

I move over by the door so I can hear Lynn coming while I type a reply.

ME: What in the hell where you thinking?

When there isn't a reply right away, I go into the closet and put on some sweatpants, a t-shirt and Nike slides. I check my phone. Still no response.

I throw some random clothes into an overnight bag and sit it on the bed.

Pacing around, I check my phone again.

Still no response.

I go over and look out the door before typing another message.

ME: I know you're up. Answer me.

I hear Lynn's footsteps so I hurry, lock the phone and sit at the foot of the bed.

"You're still here?" She asks walking back into the room.

"Can we please talk about this?"

"Who is boo?"

I sigh. "She's someone I met on the internet. Look Lynn, I didn't mean for things to get this far. You've got to believe me."

She laughs. "Goodbye Jerome."

"I told you what you asked."

"No, you told me what you think I wanted to hear."

"What else do you want?"

"I want you to be truthful because regardless of where you met her, you know her name. So, who is she?"

"What difference does her name make?" I ask standing up because I am getting annoyed.

"Oh, you're getting mad? I see your nostrils flaring. I guess you take me for a fool but let me remind you of who I am."

"I don-"

"I'm the girl from the heart of South Memphis who cooked on a one burner hot plate while washing clothes in the bath tub of a one-bedroom basement apartment. I'm the chick who walked fifteen minutes to catch a bus, the entire time I was pregnant with two of our children, just so you could get back and forward to the certification classes you needed to start OUR business. I'm the same woman who stayed up and balanced the books of the same business to keep us from going under for the first five years while sacrificing every want and need of this house. Nigga, if you think I'm about to stand here and hand it over to boo, while you play dumb; you have another thing coming."

"I told you I messed up."

"No baby, you fucked up but here's what I know for sure. You'll never play me again. See, while you were out, I took the time to go through the messages between you and boo. Those messages revealed a relationship that spans a year. Those messages revealed this isn't the first time you've had her in my bed. Those messages revealed she's more important than your wife. Those messages revealed she knows intricate parts of my husband that even I don't know. And those messages tell me that she knows all about me and my children yet you're protecting her identity which I find interesting, by the way. So, at this point, you gotta roll partna while I decide what you'll get in the divorce."

I grab my bag and walk towards the door.

"Lynn, I am so sorry. I never meant for any of this to happen."

"Yes you did, you just never meant to get caught but it's cool. I pray God have mercy on your pitiful soul."

Lynn

When Jerome leaves, I begin to snatch every stitch of cover from the bed.

"Nathaniel and Lilly!" I yell. "I need your help."

They come running from upstairs.

"Ma'am."

"Help me pull this mattress, box spring and bed frame outside."

They both look confused.

"Don't ask any questions, just help."

After about an hour, we have every piece outside on the curb.

"Mom, you do know tomorrow is Memorial Day and there is no garbage pickup, right?" Lilly says.

"I know but it'll be there when they do pickup."

"Where are you going to sleep?" Nathaniel asks.

"I'll be fine. Don't worry about me."

I walk into my bedroom and grab the covers, taking them and stuffing them into the garbage can outside. I stop and grab a piece of the wood frame of the bed that must have broken off. I don't know why. Anyway, by the time I am done, my hair is a curly ball of mess. I am sweaty and on the verge of tears but I refuse to cry.

Going back into my bedroom, I close the door, take my phone and hook it to the charger before connecting it to the Bluetooth speaker on the dresser. Pressing play on the song *Complicated,* LeAndria Johnson's voice booms through the speakers. I put it on repeat.

"Saying you love me comes easy, showing you love must be hard. My soul can't take another broken heart. Why do you say you love me, when you know you really don't mean it? Is lust the only factor cause love, I just don't see it. Love is complicated."

I look around the empty space of the room, turning around in circles as the song plays.

"So, what you waited for, love don't live here no more. I've done all I can but loving you just won't do. My

love will stand in the midst of the storm, can you hear me calling from a broken wall? Love is complicated."

I fall into the floor, sobbing from the depths of my soul.

"How could you do this Jerome?" I scream pulling at the carpet until the tips of my fingers hurt. "Why?"

"Love is complicated," sings in the background.

*****

The next morning, I open my eyes to see Lilly, Mallory and Nathaniel standing over me.

"What are y'all doing? You dang near gave me a heart attack." I ask, sitting up and rubbing my hand over my face, realizing I'm in the middle of the floor.

"Are you okay?" Nathaniel says.

"Yes, why are you asking?" I ask slowly pulling my legs up for them to sit.

"We heard you crying last night." Mallory says sounding so sad. "Are you and daddy getting a divorce?"

I look at them as the tears well up in my eyes.

"Mom, we are not babies anymore. You can be honest with us. We heard you talking to grandma and granddad yesterday." Lilly says. "And we know you and dad are having issues and he left last night with a bag."

"And now you're sleeping in the middle of an empty floor. What's going on?" Nathaniel asks as I try to move and see the cover. "We covered you up and stopped your music."

I sigh before wiping the tears and patting the floor for them to sit. "First, you all had no business eavesdropping while grown folks were talking. Secondly, whatever issues your father and I are having, we will handle. Finally, while I appreciate the fact you all are not babies anymore, stay in your place."

"We didn't mean to overstep." Lilly says. "We are just worried about you and daddy."

"We don't want you to get a divorce." Mallory cries.

"Listen guys, I am not about to lie to you. Your daddy left last night and I don't know where he went or when he's coming back. What I can tell you is, we have not made a decision about anything yet." Mallory continues to cry. "I know change is scary, but daddy and I love you and will never do anything that would hurt you. However, I need for each of you to let us handle the grown-up things and when it's time for us to talk to you all, we will. Okay?"

"Okay," they say in unison.

I stretch out my arms and they all pile in for a hug.

"Can I ask one last question?" Lilly asks when I release her.

"Sure."

"Are you really okay?"

"Sweet pea, it is not your place to worry about me. I'm the mom and it's my responsibility to make sure you all are well, healthy and happy. It's not the other way around."

"But--"

"Everything is going to be alright. Now, since I'm up, why don't we go out to get breakfast and do some school shopping before we head to moms?"

"Can I get that new purse, I showed you at the Guess store?"

"I guess so." I say trying to crack a joke, but Lilly shakes her head.

When they leave, I sigh trying to not to cry. I lay out in the floor, on my face to pray.

"Dear God, please don't allow my heart to turn to stone. Please don't allow the anger of this situation to get the best of me. And please forgive me if I do or say anything that is outside of your will. Guide me, protect me but more importantly keep my mind. Cover my children. God, this marriage was ordained by you but your word says in Hebrews 13:4, Let marriage be held in honor among all, and let the marriage bed be undefiled, for God will judge the sexually immoral and adulterous. You are the only one who can judge now. Have your way. Amen."

I get up and go about handling my morning duties and getting dressed in some shorts and a tank top. After breakfast, the kids and I go over to the Tanger Outlet Mall in Southaven, MS.

"Look, you all have money on your cards but it's only for school shopping. No video games, Nathaniel."

"Yes ma'am."

"Does everybody have their id?"

"Yes ma'am." They all say.

"Good. I will meet you all back here in a few hours. Keep your phones on."

After dropping them off, I go to Ashley Furniture.

"Good morning ma'am are you looking for anything in particular?" The young lady asks.

"A new bed. Something with a tufted headboard."

"Sure. What size and is there a particular color?"

"King and black."

"Right this way." She says leading me to the back of the store.

When I turn the corner, I see the exact one I want. "This one."

She laughs. "It is one of our most sought-after brands."

"Do you have it in stock?"

"Let me check."

While she's gone, I browse through some other items. My phone vibrates with another call from Jerome.

I decide to answer.

"What?" I say through clenched teeth. "Why are you at the house? Did you think I would sleep in that bed again? Fine. I'll drop the kids off at my parent's and meet you at the house at, um," I look at my watch, "4:30." I hang up.

"Yes ma'am, we have it in stock and it can be delivered by Wednesday." The young lady says walking up.

"Great. That's what I want."

"Don't you want to know how much it cost?" She asks with a curious look on her face.

"Nope, my husband and his mistress are paying for it?"

Her mouth forms an O, but she doesn't say anything.

"Oh, I'll need a mattress, box spring and the matching nightstands. And do you have a small tufted sofa to match?"

"I think so." She slowly says.

"I want it too."

I spend the next hour finishing paperwork. Walking out to the car, I see a note on the windshield. I look around to see if maybe it's one of those promotional flyers but when I don't notice any on other cars, I get nervous.

I take the note and open it.

Rock a bye Lynn, on your doorstop,

When the wind blows, your world will rock.

When the bough breaks, your marriage will fall,

And I'll catch Jerome, I'm having his baby after all.

-- Signed, His Mistress, Boo ❤

I stick the note in my purse before getting in my car to get the kids from the mall.

"Mom, you're not coming in?" Lilly asks when I pull up to my parent's house.

"I have something to do first. Tell grandma I'll be back in an hour."

Jerome

Sitting on the balcony of the hotel, nursing my fourth or maybe fifth Hennessey and coke, I began to think back to when Lynn and I moved into our home.

It was over fifteen years ago, almost three years after we were married. Lynn and I were living in a basement apartment we rented from this old couple we met at the hardware store. It was all God's doing because the older gentleman was trying to make some repairs on his house while Lynn and I were there to get some bug spray for this room we were paying, by the day, to stay in.

Long story short, we started talking and ended up moving into their basement apartment the same night.

We'd both graduated from college and had just gotten married. Lynn with a degree in Dance and mine in Graphic and Architectural Design. At the time, Lynn was pregnant with Lilly. We didn't have much money but we both worked odd jobs and saved every penny. We kept our credit score good and we studied and researched everything from business to home ownership programs.

In two years, we'd saved enough to purchase the land, our house sits on and secured a loan. I'd recently started Watson Construction and since my company was new, I did a lot of the work myself because building our house was used as the branding in our business.

And just like we'd prayed for, once our house was done, business started booming. The night we moved in was amazing.

"Welcome home Mr. Watson."

"What is all this?" I ask looking around the living room that is covered in candles and a rug in the middle of the floor.

"This is your housewarming gift." Lynn says, slowly walking towards me in a red negligee and heels with her eight-month pregnant stomach in front of her. "I thought

we'd christen our new home tonight before the movers deliver the furniture tomorrow."

She hands me a plastic flute, full of sparkling juice.

"Is that right? And what room did you have in mind?"

"All of them." She smiles. "That's if you can keep up."

"Oh, you got jokes."

"Well, quit talking and more action." She seductively says.

I down the drink, drop the plastic flute on the ground and begin to loosen my tie. "I think I can assist you with that Mrs. Watson."

The sound of another balcony door opening brings me out of my thoughts. My phone vibrates, no caller id, I press decline. I get up to make another drink when my phone vibrates again. I go to press decline but it's a text from Lynn.

LYNN: Keep you mistress in check.

"What?" I say to myself. I dial Lynn's number but she doesn't answer. My phone vibrates with another text. It's a picture of a note.

Rock a bye Lynn, on your doorstop,

When the wind blows, your world will rock.

When the bough breaks, your marriage will fall,

And I'll catch Jerome, I'm having his baby after all.

-- Signed, His Mistress, Boo ♥

"DAMN IT!" I say throwing my glass into the wall before falling back on the bed.

I text her.

ME: Lynn, I'm sorry.

LYNN: Yea, one sorry MFER!

ME: Are we still meeting to talk?

LYNN: Not unless you're planning to tell me who she is.

ME: I will. Just give me a chance to explain.

LYNN: Be here by 4:30 or don't bother showing up.

I look at my watch to see I have an hour.

What happened to us Jerome? We used to be so happy." I hear Lynn's voice before my mind flashes back to when I allowed things to get out of hand.

"Mr. Watson, you have a Ms. Howard here to see you."

"Ms. Howard? Do I have it on my calendar?" I ask Reanna.

"No sir, she says it's a personal matter."

"Send her in." I say looking at my watch.

When the door opens, I am shocked by the person standing there.

"Reanna, you can go ahead and leave. I plan on being here a few more hours finishing this contract and no need in the both of us wasting our Friday night."

"Is there anything you need before I go?" She asks looking at my guest up and down.

"No, I have everything. Enjoy your weekend."

I wait until she closes the door.

"Were you thrown off by the last name?" She smiles.

"I was. Please have a seat and tell me what I can do for you."

"Well, you said if there was anything I needed, I could come to you, remember?"

"I do but I was speaking in reference to construction needs."

"Oh, I thought we were passed that when our conversation changed." She said crossing her legs.

"That was a mistake."

"Was it? You didn't have to respond, remember."

"And you didn't have to send those pictures." I tell her.

"Did you like them, though?"

"Of course I did. What man wouldn't?"

"I'm not talking about any man, I'm talking about you, Mr. Watson. Did you enjoy them?"

"I did, Ms. Howard. More than I should have."

She smiles.

"And I enjoyed yours."

"I shouldn't have sent them." I say hoping my face wasn't starting to feel as red as it felt.

"Am I making you nervous?"

"What do you need, Ms. Howard. I have a lot of work to do tonight before I get home."

"You."

I smile. "Me?"

I watch as she walks around my desk.

"Yes, you sir. I need you because the heated text conversations, the phone sex and the pictures all have me needing you, papi."

She slides my chair backs, sits on the desk and spreads her legs in front of me.

"Tell me you don't want me as much as I want you." She coos.

"You know I do but this is so wrong. I'm married."

I watch as she rubs herself.

"Hmm," I moan.

"Come on papi, it'll be our secret."

"Just this one time, okay."

"Whatever you say." She smiles.

I wake up to the sound of a slamming door.

When I raise up, my head reminds me of all the drinks I've consumed. The door to the balcony is still open and it is pitch black outside.

"No, no!" I say trying to figure out where my phone is.

I jump up and begin moving the covers around and finally the phone falls out.

I grab it and press the home button. When it lights up, the phone reads … 10:02PM.

I fall to my knees, realizing I missed my chance to talk to Lynn.

THREE WEEKS LATER

Lynn

I let down my mirror and apply some lip gloss. Dropping it in my clutch, I make sure I have my id, credit card and keys before I step out the car, fix my dress and walk into the doors of The Underground.

For a Thursday night, the club was packed. I stop and survey the club then walk to the bar.

"What can I get you to drink?" The bartender asks.

"I'll take a mojito, please."

"No, fix her the club special." Mateo says to the bartender, appearing out of nowhere. He then walks over to me. "What are you doing here, mi amor? Shouldn't you be home with your husband?"

"Is that where you want me to be because I can always leave."

He gets closer and bends down pressing his lips against my ear. "If it were up to me, I want you buck naked, on my desk with your legs across my shoulders and you screaming my name but I'll settle for you sitting at my bar."

I cross my legs to prevent them from spontaneously opening. Thank God for the bartender sitting a drink in front of me. I quickly pick it up and take a sip.

"Hmm, this is good. What is it?"

"It's my secret." He says walking off.

I spend the next few hours dancing and enjoying myself. Making my way back to the bar, my phone vibrates.

I take a napkin to wipe my face and neck.

"Miss, can I get you something?" The bartender asks.

"Just water, please."

I pull my phone out to see a text in the unknown sender box. I click on it.

TEXT:

Pussy cat, pussy cat,

Where has your husband been?

He's been to my house, laying up with his queen.

Pussy cat, pussy cat,

What did he do there?

He had me screaming his name while pulling my hair.

--Signed, His Mistress, Boo ❤

I screenshot the text and send it to Jerome

ME: Control your whore.

"Hey, are you enjoying yourself?" Mateo asks in my ear.

"I'll be better if you take me back to your office." I tell him, spinning around on the bar stool.

"Are you sure, mi amor?"

"Very sure." I say spreading my legs, a little.

He takes my hand and I stand from the stool. He pushes his way through the crowd with me behind him. When we make it to his office door, he punches in a code and slides the door back for me to walk in.

I look around the office.

"It's very nice in here."

"Thank you." He says coming up behind me, close enough to feel his erection on my butt.

He keeps walking until I am pressed against his desk. I turn to face him.

"You know I've been dreaming about you since the first night you walked into my club, don't you?"

"Is that so?"

"Yes."

"Tell me about your dreams." I say smiling.

"There's been only one, every night." He says, sliding a hand under my dress to spread my legs.

I gasp.

"You come into the club in a black, fitted dress that stops right at your knees. You don't have on any panties, I can tell because there are no lines. I watch you dance all night and I get jealous as I imagine all the places the sweat gets to touch that I wish I could. In between your breasts, behind your ears and the inside of your thighs."

My eyes close as his hands roam.

"You can feel my eyes on you so you dance just for me, moving and touching yourself, arousing the parts of me that are longing to feel the insides of you. I wait until you walk out of the bathroom, I grab your hand and pull you into my office where I bend you over my desk and devour you; first with my hands. Like this." He says rubbing his hands against my lady.

I moan some more.

"I enter you, one finger at a time, like this."

I open my mouth but the words get caught in my throat when his fingers begin to play me like a piano.

My moan gets louder.

"I watch you--"

"Boss, you're needed on the floor. There's a medical emergency." A male says knocking on the door. "Boss, you in there?"

He grunts before releasing me.

"Please don't leave."

I wait until he walks out before I stand and fix my dress. I walk into the bathroom to get a wet paper towel. Coming out, I see his phone light up on the desk.

I go over to it and press the home button.

No lock code.

I see pictures of me on the dance floor. I pick up the phone and go through his other pictures and see a lot of them are of me. I pull out my phone and take a few screenshots before I go through his messages but there are only a few taking about the club. I am about to go to his contact list but I hear someone in the hall. I hurriedly lock the phone and put it back where it was.

There is a door in his office. I open it and it leads to a parking lot.

I get into my car and lock the doors before pressing the start button. Making the thirty-minute trip home, I am overloaded by my thoughts. I finally pull in the garage. Getting inside the house, I lock up and set the alarm before running down the hall. Stripping out of my clothes, I turn the water on for the shower and step inside, not waiting for it to get warm. Once the cold water hits my face, I burst into tears.

"God, I am sorry. Please forgive me for my thoughts and actions while you strengthen me not to give in to temptation. Please God. I don't want to repay sin for sin. Forgive me. Oh God, forgive me."

Jerome

"Hello."

Crying.

"Hello."

"Why are you treating me like this? I love you and I need you."

"Mattie, please stop the dramatics and leave me alone."

"WHY?" She yells. "You're not at home anyway so why can't I see you? I need you!"

"You don't need me, you need help. Stop calling me." I release the call and leave my phone in the truck before walking into the foreman's office.

"Hey Jerome, I wasn't expecting you today. Is something wrong?" Lee asks when I walk in.

"No, everything is good. I had some time on my hand, so I decided to come by and check out the progress. I had a meeting with the Addison Group and they are pleased with all the work you and your team have done so far."

"Man, that's great to hear. Thank you for entrusting me with such a big task. I can't lie though, I thought you'd be more hands on." He says.

"I know but I have so much going on."

"Business or personal?" He asks.

"Personal that could ultimately affect my business."

"I'm sorry to hear that. You want to talk about it?" Lee asks.

"I really messed up and it could cost me losing my wife."

"Jerome, marriage is a lot of work and we sometimes mess up at it but man if your marriage is worth saving, save it because you and Lynn have been together too long to let it all go now. However, if you know you aren't willing to be the husband and man Lynn needs, let her go. You owe her more than just keeping her for the sake of keeping her."

"I don't know how to fix it though. She won't even talk to me."

"Have you stopped talking and start praying?" He asks. "Prayers can do things we can't. Jerome, you're my boss so I will never get in your business where it doesn't pertain to me but man, I know what it feels like to be in your position. My wife and I went through a period of separation that almost ended in divorce and our only saving grace was prayer and fasting."

"Did it have to do with infidelity because that's where we are?"

"No, for us, we grew apart but it doesn't mean your marriage can't be fixed. First, you must start with honesty. It's the hardest step and the most challenging. It will make you think you can't get pass it but you can if you put in the work. A lot of work. Are you up for it?"

"Lee, I will do whatever I have too to keep my wife, but I don't know if she is willing."

"I take it, you were the one who cheated?"

I nod.

"Brother, she is going to kill you." He laughs.

"I already know."

"Look, I don't have all the answers but I do know restoration is available but you have to give Lynn the space to heal. There is going to be times when she will say and act like you're the most disgusting human on earth but it'll be her emotions because let's face it, you hurt her and you hurt her bad."

"I know man. I never meant too. I love that woman." I say.

"Tell her that and everything else whether it's good, bad or indifferent because you owe her that."

He puts his hands on my shoulder and before he removes it, he begins to pray.

"Dear God, I am coming to you on behalf of my brother who needs you. God, hear this prayer and give him the words needed to repair what has been broken. Then God, forgive him of his faults and strengthen him to forgive himself for we all fall short of your glory. Yet God we thank you for grace that covers us and for mercy that keeps us. Restore what you have ordained, if it is your will. Amen."

"Amen and thank you brother." I tell him.

"No thanks needed. I'm only doing for you what someone else did for me and that is to pour back in what you feel you've lost spiritually. Hold on," he says going into his wallet and handing me a card.

"Who is this?"

"Her name is Dr. Savannah Mitchell."

"A therapist?"

"She is more of a spiritual guide. You and Lynn should talk to her."

"Thanks brother. I'll think about it."

I end up staying at the construction site for a few hours before heading back to the office.

It's after four, when I make it back.

Reanna isn't at her desk so I rush into my office to change clothes because I am sweaty from working. I walk in and see a purse sitting on the couch. I hear voices so I walk around the corner. I smile before walking up and putting my hand on the small of her back.

She turns around "Oh, I am so sorry." I say feeling embarrassed. "I thought you were my wife."

"Mr. Watson, you forgot about your meeting with Ms. Gable?" Reanna asks to dissolve the weirdness now looming in the air.

"You looked just liked my wife from behind. I am so sorry." I say again.

She laughs. "It's okay."

"And yes Reanna. I totally forgot. Please give me a few minutes to change my shirt."

It takes about ten minutes for me to wash up and change.

I join Reanna and Sydney in the design room.

"Mr. Watson, Ms. Gable is here to have some renovations done on her home. She has a smaller room, next to her master that she would like converted into a walk-in closet. She also wants it to have an access point from her room."

"She is correct, and I bought the plans to the house, if you need them." Sydney says.

"Great, let me take a look." I tell her getting up to spread them out on the table. "Okay, hmm, well I don't see an issue in making these rooms adjoining. This wall here is not load bearing so we can add a door here to give you access from the bedroom. We can keep this window but update it and everything else will be cosmetic relating to the design changes you desire. Those I will leave up to you and Reanna as she is our staff designer. As for today, I cannot give you an estimate until I've had a chance to do a thorough inspection of the room. However, you and Reanna can look at samples of designs that can give us a ballpark of where you would like to be, budget wise." I tell her.

"Sounds good."

"Great. I will leave you ladies to it. Reanna, I have a call to take, in my office but let me know if you need me."

"Yes sir."

-tapping on the door-

I look up to see Sydney in the door. "Hey, did you all finish up everything?"

"Not quite but I told her I'll wait until you actually come to the house before I finalize plans because I want you to add some shelving to the closet."

"No problem. Did you schedule a date and time?"

"We did, for Thursday."

"Great, I'll see you then."

"Cool, you have my number if you need to reach me before then. It was good seeing you Jerome."

Lynn

"Mattie?" I call out, walking inside the front door.

"Come in and lock the door behind you."

I do before walking around the corner to the living room.

"Hey," she says coming over to give me a hug.

"You have a beautiful house. I didn't know you'd lived this close to me. You've been keeping secrets."

"Well, I have been trying to get you over here for girl's night, remember."

"Vaguely." I say.

"Whatever." She laughs, "Come on in."

"Where's everybody?"

"It's just you and me tonight because everybody else backed out at the last minute. I didn't tell you because there was no sense ruining our night." She says going over to the bar area. "You want wine or something stronger?"

"Give me something stronger."

I get ready to sit but Mattie stops me.

"No, don't sit because were going out to the backyard. This way."

"Mattie, oh my God, this screened porch is beautiful." I tell her walking around it.

"Thank you. It was done by a company the realtor suggested and the guy did an amazing job. He is very skilled with his hands." She replies. "Anyway, sit and tell me what's going on with you."

Before I can say anything, her phone rings. She rolls her eyes and then answers. "What's up E? No, I'm busy. Why? No, I am not about to have this conversation with you again. No. NO! "Look Erica," Mattie pauses holding the phone away from her ear. "Are you done? Well, you aren't but I am. Goodbye."

"Wow. Is everything okay between you and Erica?"

"Erica is pregnant." She blurts.

"But I thought the two of you were together."

"So did I but apparently she's been having an affair."

"With who?"

"She says she was artificially inseminated, but I don't believe her."

"Why not?"

"It's expensive and there is a process you have to go through with hormones and such. I know because we were supposed to do it together, so we did all the research then suddenly, she pops up pregnant. Anyway, until she can be honest with me, I am done."

"I feel you on that. No need of wasting time with a cheater. We are too good for them."

"Amen." She says. "Wait, what do you mean we?"

"Jerome is cheating too."

She laughs. "Girl stop lying. Not Mr. Deacon of the year."

I sip my drink.

"Lynn are you serious?"

"Yep, the bastard has been cheating for over a year. I hope he gets blue balls."

She looks at me and we both laugh.

"Damn, is nobody faithful anymore?" She asks.

"Nope." I say downing my drink.

"Do you smoke?"

"May as well, I don't have anybody to go home too nor a job to get up for."

She sits her glass down before grabbing the cigar from the ash tray. "What are you going to do?"

"About what?"

"Jerome." She asks rolling the cigar.

"I don't know. Right now, I am pissed that he will not be truthful about who she is. It's like he's protecting her."

"Maybe he's protecting you." She says licking the cigar.

"Protecting me from what? The damage was done when he broke our vows. That's why I told him to pack his crap and go while I threw him the deuces."

"You aren't worried about losing everything?" She asks lighting the cigar and taking a pull.

"Losing what? My momma didn't raise a fool. Suga, all we own is fifty-one percent ownership of Lynn Watson."

She gets choked.

"Are you okay?"

She coughs and waves her hand before laughing.

"Dang girl, I didn't know you had it like that."

"I don't have it like anything because that decision wasn't made for a time such as this. It was made because Jerome loved me enough then to know I'd never take advantage of him. We built that company while we lived in a rented basement apartment and I be damned if I let somebody else reap the benefits. Anyway, can we change the subject?"

She shakes her head and passes me the cigar.

For the next few hours and after a few more drinks and a couple of drags from Mattie's cigar; I am feeling good. We go back into the living room and

Mattie puts on some music. We are up dancing when her hands begin to roam over my body.

At first, I don't stop her but then she pulls me in for a kiss.

"Whoa. Mattie, what are you doing?"

"I'm making you forget your worries."

She grabs my hand and I allow her to lead me to her bedroom.

*****

I roll over and jump up when I don't recognize where I am.

"Where are you going?"

I turn at the sound of Mattie's voice. She laughs.

"Girl, I forgot where I was." I look down and see I only have on my shirt and panties. "Oh my God, did we--"

"Heck no. I will never take advantage of an intoxicated vagina." She says.

"Oh, thank God."

"Well damn." She says.

"I'm sorry, I didn't mean--"

"I know what you meant."

I raise my arm and realize my watch is dead.

"What time is it?"

"Five minutes after ten."

"Dang, my kids must be worried sick." I begin to frantically look around for my pants.

"Slow down." Mattie says. "You took your pants off in the bathroom. I laid them on the arm of the chair."

"Girl, I can't remember the last time I've been drunk. I hope I didn't do anything embarrassing."

"Does making a few videos count?" She asks with a straight face.

"Oh my God, what did I do? Please tell me it was nothing stupid."

She burst into laughing.

"I'm just playing." She says trying to catch her breath. "You should see your face."

I throw a pillow at her. "How are you so bright eyed?"

"I can handle my liquor missy."

"Whatever." I say putting my jeans on.

"Do you need me to make you some coffee or anything before you go? I think I have some eggs and bread for toast."

"No, I'm good but thank you for last night. I had a great time."

"You don't have to thank me. That's what friends are for, right?" She asks.

"Right."

Jerome

"Are y'all ready?"

"Almost." Lilly yells.

I stand in the hallway waiting on the kids to get dressed so we can go to lunch, since they missed breakfast.

Nathaniel comes out first.

"Where's your sisters?"

He shrugs.

"Girls come on. It'll be dinner by the time you're ready."

Ten minutes later, they come running out.

"It took all that time for y'all to throw on those little shorts?"

"Dad, this is called fashion."

I shake my head.

We finally get out to the truck.

"You think mom can join us for lunch?" Lilly asks.

"I don't know. You can ask, if you want." I tell them.

"I'm calling her." Mallory states, having already dialed the number.

"Hey Mallory."

"Hey mom, I was seeing if you wanted to meet us for lunch."

"Um," she hesitates. "Where?"

"AC's Steakhouse." I holler out.

"Are you headed there now?"

"Yes."

"Okay, I'll meet you there in thirty."

When Mallory releases the call, I smile.

Thirty minutes later, Lynn comes walking through the doors in a flowing maxi dress, flat sandals and her shoulder length, natural curls bouncing. It seemed as if all eyes were on her. I stand up to greet her.

"Wow mom, you look amazing." Nathaniel compliments her.

"Thank you sir." She says. "Hi Jerome."

I didn't realize I was staring until she called my name.

"Hey. Nathaniel is right. You look beautiful." I step back to allow her to slide into the booth.

"Thank you. Where are the girls?" She asks once she's seated.

"They went to the bathroom."

"Man, you smell good. Is that--"

"Grape body oil from The Bubble Bistro." She finishes.

I close my eyes to get from getting aroused. Dang, this lady pulled out all the punches.

"Mommy!" Mallory sings all the way to the table.

"Hey ladies, you both look very pretty." I tell them.

"Thanks, and so do you. Where you headed on a date or something?" Mallory asks.

"No, I was home." She says looking at the menu.

The waiter comes and we order our drinks and food at the same time. The kids are telling us about their recent trip, with their grandparents. I look over and can't believe we are having an enjoyable afternoon.

My phone vibrates.

I open a text from an unsaved number.

I click on the picture and it shows Mateo whispering in Lynn's ear at a bar. I feel my blood heating up. I scroll to the next one and it's of them walking through the club, hand in hand. The next is her walking into his office.

"Dad!"

"Huh? What did you say?"

"The food is here." Mallory tells me.

"Are you okay?" Lynn asks me.

"Yea, I'm good."

I barely touch my food, so I have the waiter pack it to go. I send the kids to my truck to get their bags while I stop Lynn to talk.

"What's up?" She asks.

"Are you having an affair?"

She laughs. "Are you serious?"

"Very. Are you sleeping with that Spanish dude from the club?" I ask with my jaws clenched so tight together.

She steps a little closer to me. "Jerome, if I am or am not sleeping with him, it is of no concern to you. It's been over a month since I caught you and you've yet to be honest with me. So, from where I'm standing, you don't get to ask me about anything I do. Thank you for lunch though."

When she goes to walk off I grab her arm.

"Is this really what we're about to do?" She asks looking from me to my arm.

"Just tell me? Please Lynn."

"Why would I do that? Oh, does it hurt for you to think about somebody else getting what used to belong to you? Does it hurt the baby to think somebody else may be licking his pudding? Well, too bad boo. You made this bed."

She snatches her arm from me and walks to her car.

"Children tell your dad goodbye."

I pace around the outside of the restaurant for a few minutes before making a call.

"No, I'm not good and I really need to talk to you. Yes sir, I can come now."

`Back door opening`

I look up to see Lynn's dad, Frank walking out. He hands me a beer.

"I messed up." I say before he even sits down.

"I heard. You want to talk about it?" He asks.

"I had an affair. I don't know why but I did. Lynn has been everything to me since I was seventeen.

SEVENTEEN. I never looked at another woman in that way."

"Stop lying."

"Huh?" I ask looking at Frank.

"Stop lying because we've all looked at other women. Say you've never acted on it until now."

"I've never acted on it until now. What's wrong with me?"

"Son, you're human. Look Jerome, I would be lying if I sat here and berated you for a mistake most men make. Does it mean I condone what you did? Hell no because you hurt my daughter but you need to figure out where to go from here." He says.

"I don't know what to do."

"Start by being honest and let the pieces fall where they may because it is only then you can pick them up and rebuild. You know this, you're a builder."

"Yea but how can you rebuild with missing pieces?" I ask.

"You make new ones to fit where the old ones are missing. However, you must be sure the new pieces can make the old thing look the same or better. If not, you may as well scrap the old thing and build anew."

"That's what I'm afraid of."

"But you'll survive."

"Dad, this girl has been a part of me since I was seventeen."

"Yet you found it easy to give away something that should have been sacredly hers."

"I made a mistake."

"I know but that mistake may have cost you the life as you know it."

Lynn

Sitting at home, on the couch binge watching the Hallmark Channel. Lilly is gone with her best friend Lexie for the Fourth of July holiday. Mallory is at my parent's house because they promised to take her shopping for fireworks and Nathaniel is spending the night at his friend's house down the street.

The doorbell rings.

I get up and see that it's Jerome.

I open the door.

"The kids aren't here."

"Good because I need to talk to you. Can I please come in?"

I turn and walk back into the den, pausing the TV before sitting back on the couch and covering my legs with the blanket.

Jerome sits across from me but doesn't say anything for a few minutes.

"Did you come here to talk or stare?"

"Are you sleeping with the Mateo dude?"

"Get out."

"I won't be upset, just tell me. I already know because somebody sent me pictures of the two of you together but I want to hear it from you."

I exhale, heavily. "You had me pause my movie for this?" I tell him, throwing the blanket from my legs and standing up. "Get out."

"Lynn--"

"No Jerome! You will not come here and question my faithfulness to you when you're the reason we are in this position to begin with. As a matter of fact, you don't get to question me, at all, when you've had a chick in my bed, not once but twice. No boo, you don't get to play the victim. Not now, not ever so put one foot in front of the other and get out of this house!"

"I CHEATED!" He blurts.

I stop and look at him.

"I know you cheated stupid. Question is, who did you cheat with?"

He drops his head.

"Like I thought. Until you are ready to tell me the truth of who she is, don't come back."

"I cheated with Mattie." He somberly whispers, not looking in my direction.

I fall back onto the couch.

"I'm sorry. I thought I heard you say--repeat what you just said."

"Lynn, I've made a huge mistake but you have to know it was never my intent for any of this to happen."

"Save all that, who did you say?" I question again.

"The person I've been having an affair with is Mattie."

I laugh.

"Mattie Green? The one who goes to church with us? The one I've been hanging with the last few weeks. The same Mattie who we've known for over a year? That Mattie?"

"Yes."

"Mattie with the black hair, my height and with the cross tattoo on her wrist?"

"Yeah."

"Mattie with-"

"Yes Lynn that Mattie!" He yells.

I open my mouth but nothing comes out. It takes a minute but my voice finally comes back.

"You dirty mother--of all the women in Memphis, Mississippi and Arkansas; you had to screw somebody in our church? A woman I've seen almost every Sunday for the last fifty-two weeks? Why her?" I ask, anger starting to build in my belly.

"Over a year ago I went to a house to do an estimate for some renovations. She'd just moved to the area and bought her house and needed some work done. After the job was complete, she, well we started texting each other. It started off harmless, at first but eventually our texts turned sexually." He explains.

"I read them but you still haven't answered, why her?"

"One night, she showed up at my job and we had sex. Since then, we've engaged in sex on multiple occasions and--"

"She's been in our home." I say wiping the tears. "Not only that, you've made me look like a fool. This girl smiles in my face, holds my hand at altar calls and sits next to me in bible studies knowing she's screwing my husband. You though! You allow the barefaced disrespect because you didn't stop it by keeping your whore in check. Why Jerome? What have I done to make you hate me enough to do this?"

"Baby, please believe me, it was nothing you did or didn't do."

My right leg is starting to shake and I begin to rub my hands together. "Oh, did you think that's what I was asking? Jerome, I've been everything to you. I would have done just about anything you'd asked, within reason and you know it so I don't take the blame for you sticking your funky penis in somebody else. Let's face it, had you asked, I probably would have been incline to bring something new to our marriage bed but you never gave me the option. Instead, you took it upon yourself to sneak and eat from the forbidden tree and now you have to pay for your sin."

"I know and nothing I can say or do can make it up to you."

"You're damn right! I must be the biggest idiot to not have seen this." I get up and begin to pace around the living room. "She came on to me at the club, the night of my birthday and I told you about it. Not that I had too but I did because the way she touched me, had me thinking of doing something crazy. You still said nothing. I went to her, a few nights ago and she acted genuinely concerned about me. She said nothing. I drank, smoked and danced with her. I even fell asleep next to her, in her bed, probably the one you have shared with her before. Y'all still said nothing. This woman knows how you taste, the feel of your hands and the sounds you make when you climax because she's been the one doing all the things I should be. How could I have been so stupid?"

I cry. "She's been around our children. I'm going to be sick," I rush to the hall bathroom and empty my stomach contents into the toilet, wishing I could flush my feelings and memories, of the past twenty years with it.

I can't.

I sit there hugging the toilet willing God to make the pain stop.

Jerome

I run to the linen closet and grab a towel, wetting it at the sink before handing it to Lynn.

She flushes the toilet before sitting with her back against the wall.

"I am so sorry Lynn."

She covers her face.

"Do you love her like you told her you did?" She asks after removing the towel.

"No, I only love you."

"You are a liar because this isn't love Jerome. Love is talking to me first before reacting. If you wanted to experience something different, why not talk to me first? Maybe we could have experienced it, together, in our marriage bed but instead you go out and cheat with a woman we know. Is she the only one?"

"Yes."

Lynn chuckles. "I don't believe you but okay."

She tries to get up from the floor and when I try to help her, she pushes me away.

"Don't touch me." She says hitting me once and then over and over. "I don't even know who you are anymore."

I let her get a few punches in until I grab her and pull her into me.

"Lynn, baby stop."

"Why did you do this to us after I have given you all of me? If I wasn't enough, you should have told me. You didn't have to hurt me like this."

"I never meant to hurt you."

She pushes away from me. "Yes you did! Every time you met up for sex, you meant to hurt me. Every time you allowed her or whoever to suck your musty penis, you meant to hurt me. Every time you allowed her into our marital bed, you meant to hurt me. So stop lying. Admit your truth Jerome."

"I messed up!" I scream. "You were the only woman I'd been with since I was seventeen and I didn't know what another woman felt or taste like so I got caught up. I reacted from my flesh, but you must know that I'm sorry for the way I have behaved. I allowed curiosity to overshadow my covenant with you and I am sorry."

"You don't think I know those feelings? Negro, you've been my only sexual partner for just as long, yet I've never acted on the urges to want someone else. Instead I came to you, my husband and I told you I wanted to spice up our marriage bed. You know what you did? You laughed. You made me feel like a fool for buying lingerie when you have an account set up for her to buy it. I try to do things to you, husbands and wives should do but you said no only to turn around and do the exact same thing with her. Did you ever stop to think about asking me?"

"Asking you what?"

"For what you needed." I state. "With all the possibilities available, you didn't have to cheat Jerome because I would have been willing to give you a plus one. Hell, maybe even two. All you had to do was ask."

She says walking out of the bathroom and into the bedroom, slamming the door.

I go back into the living room and sit on the couch because I cannot leave things like this.

After two hours, I go to check on Lynn. I tap on the door but she doesn't say anything. I slowly open it and because it's still kind of early, the light from the window is shining into the room. I see her laying on the bed.

I push the door open and take in the room. It has been completely redone in the two months I've been gone. I knew she'd removed the furniture but she also had the walls repainted and pictures replaced.

I cannot lie, it looks good.

I take the comforter and pull it from what used to be my side and fold it over her. She moans a little and I can tell she's been crying. I rub her face before going over to sit on the couch, in front of the window.

She has a journal laying there. I pick it up and put it down but then I pick it up again. I sit back on the couch, closer to the light and open it up.

"I woke up the other night reaching for Jerome but he wasn't there. I talked myself out of crying but it did no good because I cried anyway. Don't get me wrong, I am not crying because I believe any of this is my fault, baby I am a bomb of a wife but my tears are from a place of pain. I wish he would have just talked to me because I would have rather given him permission than for him to do this."

I wipe the tears that are falling and flip a few pages, stopping at her last entry.

"I heard one of the children outside of my door but they didn't knock. I know it was Nathaniel because it was Tuesday. Tuesday is his day. They don't think I know it but they have been taking turns checking on me, at night to make sure I'm not crying. Lilly has Monday, Nathaniel has Tuesday, Mallory has Wednesday and then they start over. LOL! It's the sweetest thing but it also breaks my heart. Ugh Jerome makes me sick for putting us in this position. I know we will have to talk with them soon but I don't even know what I want to do at this point. I love my husband and twenty years is a long time to just throw it away but I

wonder if we matter to him anymore. If we did, he would have been honest, right?"

"Jerome?" Lynn calling my name causes me to jump. "What are you doing?"

"I wanted to make sure you were okay."

"I am, please leave my house because I don't have the energy to hear any more of your lies."

"Can--" I stop myself and do what she asks.

Walking back up front, I turn on the alarm and lock the front door behind me.

Lynn

Doorbell ringing

Mattie opens the door and her eyes widen at the shock of me standing on her doorstep.

"Hey Lynn, what's up?"

"Who am I talking to right now, Mattie or His Mistress Boo with the heart?"

Her eyes widen. "What are you talking about?" She asks, folding her arms.

"Why would you pretend to be my friend knowing you were screwing my husband?"

"I'm sorry Lynn. I never meant to become friends with you."

I chuckle. "Oh, so you meant to fall in love with my husband?"

"Well yeah. He's good looking, successful and great in bed. Who wouldn't?" She shrugs.

"What about his family?"

"Look, I'm sorry to break up what y'all had but it's about time for a change, don't you think. Besides, I am not the one who should have been thinking about the family, he should. I'm just glad he finally told you."

"You're just glad he finally--" Before I even finish the sentence I drag her out the door, down the steps and into the front yard where I commence to beating her ass.

"Hey! Y'all stop that." A woman says screaming while a dog is barking. "Lady get off her, I'm calling the police."

A few seconds later someone is pulling me by the arm.

"Ma'am stop. What are you doing? The police are on the way." She says.

"Good, I'll wait for them." I say fixing my ponytail and clothes.

A few minutes later, I hear sirens. A few other neighbors tend to Mattie while I stand propped up next to the garage.

"Ma'am, I need you to put your hands behind your back." A female officer says pointing in my direction.

"Sure thing." I say.

She places the handcuffs on me, walks me over to the car and opens the door; sitting me in but doesn't close the door.

"Ma'am, what are you doing here fighting?" She asks pulling out the pad to make a report.

"She's big mad that I'm screwing her husband." Mattie yells from behind her.

"Ma'am, I'm not talking to you. Be quiet." The officer says looking at Mattie.

"Officer, the whore is correct in that she *was* screwing my husband but this fight isn't about that. Her getting HER ASS WHIPPED is due to the blatant disrespect of being in my face while doing it."

"I sure did, so what? I would have slept with you too had you let me." She laughs.

"I am not going to tell you again." The officer says to Mattie before turning back to me. "What's your name?"

"Lynn Watson."

"Lynn about to be divorced Watson." Mattie yells before laughing.

The officer presses something on the pad, puts it back in her pocket and grabs me from the car.

"That's right take her to jail!" Mattie yells. "Bye Lynn. I'll be sure to kiss our husband tonight."

"Turn around ma'am." The officer says before removing the handcuffs. "You're free to go. She deserved every punch she received. Have a great night."

"Wait, you can't do that!" Mattie screams. "I want to press charges for assault."

Her neighbors are looking at her and shaking their heads.

"You saw her assault me, didn't you?" She asks looking at them.

"Lady, go to hell." One of them says before walking off.

The officer waits until I get into my car and I pull off giving Mattie the middle finger.

I make it home and storm into the house.

"Mom," Mallory calls out. "Are you okay?"

"Yes, I'm fine. Can you order pizza for dinner while I take a shower?"

I spend the rest of the night eating pizza and watching movies with Mallory and Nathaniel. I only had a few cuts on my hands, but they aren't noticeable. I get a cramp in my stomach that causes me to cringe.

"Mom are you okay?" Lilly asks

"Yea, this pizza isn't agreeing--" I jump up and run down the hall to the bathroom, closing the door and dashing for the toilet.

"Mom?"

"I'm okay," I say once I am done.

"You sure? I can call dad."

"No, I'm okay. Just give me a minute."

Once I am done, I open the door to Mallory's worried face.

"I am fine, I promise but I'm going to bed. Turn on the alarm and make sure the house is locked up."

I leave her in the hall before walking to my bedroom where I kneel beside the bed and say my prayers before getting under the cover.

Jerome

Two Weeks Later

Eeny, meeny, miny, moe;

You don't get to decide when I'm not needed anymore.

Eeny, meeny, miny, moe;

You might want to be careful, opening the door.

"Mr. Watson, Detective Gaiters is here." Reanna says over the intercom.

"Please show him in." I tell her before printing off the latest email from Mattie. She has been calling, texting and now emailing nonstop.

I stand up as the door opens.

"Marcus, thank you for coming man."

"Of course, it sounded important. My apologies for keeping you waiting but with the crime in

Memphis, I hardly ever get a chance to break away. What's going on?"

I grab the sheet of paper off the printer and hand it to him. He sits in the chair, in front of my desk and starts to read the email.

"Wow, who is this from?" He asks.

"Someone I was having an affair with."

He looks at me. "Dude, you cheated on Lynn? Y'all been together since like sixth grade?"

"Yea and cheating has been the worst mistake of my life too."

"Who is this chick? Is she somebody we went to school with?"

"No. Her name is Mattie Green. I met her over a year ago when she needed some work done at her house. She was new to Memphis, so she would text occasionally but then one thing led to another and we started having an affair."

"Does Lynn know?" He inquires.

"Yea and if things aren't bad enough, Mattie also goes to church with us."

"Brother, you were that careless to do it with somebody who has access to your wife and home? Jerome, that's foul."

"I know Marcus, I messed up."

"We both know you did more than that but I am not here to judge because we all make mistakes. However, you need to get a paper trail started because these kinds of domestic situations never end well. And I hate to be the bearer of more bad news, but you and your family are in more danger now than you ever were before."

"What do I need to do?"

"First, let me do some digging on this chick then I'll go and speak with her, to see where her head is and let her know you're considering legal action. In the meantime, contact the Shelby County Crime Victims Centers and they can tell you the best course of action, which maybe an order of protection."

"Do you think this will work?"

"It will either make her back off or set her off. You need to be prepared for both."

I sigh. "Thank you brother."

He stands up.

"Don't thank me yet because this may get worse before it gets better. Be careful man and keep any and everything she sends. I wouldn't speak with her unless you are able to record the calls. And I'm praying for you and Lynn. If y'all don't make it, I know for sure there is no hope for me ever getting married." He laughs. "I'll be in touch."

Getting back to my desk, my cell phone vibrates.

NO CALLER ID.

I press decline.

Some minutes later, Reanna buzzes.

"Mr. Watson, you have a call on line one. She says her name is Leotha Gray and she goes to church with you."

I pause trying to remember the name.

"Mr. Watson?"

"Send her through Reanna." I press the speaker. "This is Jerome."

"Is this what it takes for you to answer the phone?"

"Mattie, I asked you to stop calling my place of business."

"Then you should answer your phone."

"No, you should stop calling."

"You don't get to decide when this is over!" She screams. "If you think I am about to bow out gracefully, think again." She says.

"This is not a game Mattie, this is my life and right now it's in turmoil. All I am asking is for time to figure things out."

She laughs. "Time? Negro, you've had a year to figure things out. My patience is thin but tell you what. I'll give you until the end of the day to figure out what you want to do."

"I don't move to the beat of your drum." I tell her.

"I suggest you start. For your sake."

Mattie

I hang up the phone in Jerome's face.

"Ms. Anderson are you sure you don't want to test drive the truck before we finish the paperwork?" The man asks.

"Yes, I'm sure. What else do you need from me?"

"Just your driver's license and a check--"

"I only have cash."

"Cash works. The total is $2787.99"

I pull the envelope from my purse and count of the money.

"Is this going to take much longer? I need to get on the road before it gets dark." I tell him, fixing my wig and glasses.

"Thirty minutes at the most. I have the truck in the back now, getting detailed and filled with gas."

"Thanks Ralph. You've been a lifesaver."

An hour later, I am headed home. When I get a short distance from the car lot, I roll the window down, snatch off the wig and glasses and throw them out.

Looking at the time, Jerome has two more hours to call me before I set my plan into motion.

I connect my phone to the Bluetooth to play Tamar Braxton's song, *If I Don't Have You*. When the music starts, I fast forward to my part and prepare myself to sing very loud.

"Looking at my phone but you ain't even call. I put it in a drawer cause I wanna be right next to you. If you wanna talk, baby come on through before it's all done. Tell me I'm your only one. Baby, baby call me crazy cause I know without you I won't be no good. When the latch on my heart comes a loose, you should know if I don't have you. Rocks me to the core, I can't love no more if I don't have you. Know I'm done for sure, nobody worth fighting for. I'll tear down these walls that's on my life, I'll lose my mind if I don't have you."

My phone rings and I get excited but it's only Erica.

"What do you want?" I bark into the phone.

"Where are you?"

"Why?"

"Look, I know you're supposedly mad at me, but a detective came by looking for you." She says.

"A detective? For what?"

"Something to do with Jerome. He wouldn't give me much information, but he left his card for you to call him."

"Whatever throw it away." I tell her.

"Mattie, what have you done?"

"Nothing. Not yet at least."

"Mattie, please don't do anything stupid over a penis when there are plenty more out there. Leave him alone because you can't make him choose you. He has the police involved, please Mattie." She whines.

"You're the last person to talk about leaving a married man alone. I got to go."

I end the call and the music starts back but I grab the phone and dial Jerome's number.

"You've reached the voicemail of Jerome Watson with Watson Construction. Please leave a detailed message at the tone and I will return your call as soon as possible."

BEEP

"Oh, you got the police involved? Really Jerome? You're a coward! DO YOU HEAR ME? You're a coward and--"

"If you're satisfied with your message, press one. If you--"

I press the button to end the call. "UGH!! You will not get away with this Jerome Watson."

I turned the music back up and punch the gas.

Lynn

Music playing

"This kind of matter won't let me sleep. It's got me up, flipping the channels on my TV. This kind of sadness won't let me cry. It's got me up pacing the hall, each and every night."

The treadmill slows down. I turn my music off and reach for my towel.

"Your voice is beautiful."

I smile but then roll my eyes when I realize its Mateo. I press stop and step off the treadmill.

"How long have you been standing there?" I ask after taking a sip of my water.

"Not long. Where have you been? I haven't seen you here in a few weeks or at the club. Is everything okay?" He questions.

"Stay away from me Mateo." I try to walk away but he grabs me.

"Let me go or I'll scream."

"What's wrong?" He asks.

"Why do you have pictures of me in your phone?"

"Oh."

"Yes, oh. Why?" I ask again.

It's not what you think mi amor."

"Mane cut that Spanish bull crap with me. You're not going to even ask how I found out."

"I have cameras in my office so I know how you knew."

"Yet you still had the audacity to stand in my face like you've done nothing. Typical. Tell me one thing, who put you up to taking pictures of me and why?"

He doesn't say anything.

"It's cool because if you have cameras then you know I took pictures of everything and I plan on taking them to the police."

"What can they do?" He asks stopping in front of me. "Taking pictures isn't illegal. You were in my club, remember."

"Yea, you're right." I say sounding defeated. "But who knows what the police will find when they get a tip about underage drinking and drugs being sold on the premises. So, good luck because you're going to need it by the time I'm done." I say getting ready to walk off before he grabs my arm.

"Wait."

I snatch my arm from him. "What am I waiting for? Why do you have a phone full of pictures of me, when I've only been to your club twice? I don't know you and you shouldn't know me so tell me what's going Mateo?"

He motions for me to follow him over to a corner.

"It was Mattie." He says looking around.

"Mattie? Why would she put you up to this?"

"She's my sister."

"She's your what?" I ask with shock written all over my face.

"My sister and she threatened to take my club from me if I didn't do what she said."

"You better tell me everything and I mean everything, right now." I demand.

He blows before beginning to speak. "She came to me, a few months back with a plan to seduce you. She said you were sleeping with the man she wanted and the only way she could get him away from you, was to prove you were cheating. Once she did, he would leave you and be with her."

"What?" I say louder than I expected, causing people to look at me. After a few seconds, I turn back to him. "Did any of this cockamamie plan sound like a good idea to you? Did it ever occur to you that your sister is crazy and that this man she was getting me away from is my husband?" I ask him.

"None of this makes sense which is why I wouldn't go along with it."

"I'm not following because you seem to be going along with it to me."

"I wasn't until you showed up at my club for your birthday. Mattie came over to the bar and pointed you out then she sent me over to your table to introduce myself."

"Wait, how'd you know I would be there that night?"

"I didn't. I assume Mattie had invited you."

"No, I saw the flyer on Facebook and after my husband pissed me off—wait, do you think Jerome was in on it too?" I ask him.

He shrugs. "I don't know but I wouldn't be surprised because Mattie has a way of getting people to do whatever she wants."

"What were you supposed to do that night?"

"Slip something in your drink and have sex with you in my office. I have cameras and it would have been recorded. When I wouldn't do it, she took matters into her own hands, hence the bathroom."

"This doesn't make sense. What does she have on you?"

"My club. When I started The Underground, I did so with some bad investors and Mattie knows this. Most of the money is clean now but she can destroy everything I've worked hard to build, and I cannot allow her to ruin this for me."

"So, you allow her to ruin my life instead?"

"I didn't know what else to do." He says rubbing his head.

"Is that why you showed up at the gym the next day?" I ask and he nods. "The gas station?"

"The gym was set up but the gas station was purely coincidental. Lynn, I'm so sorry. I wanted to tell you and I was going to." He says.

"When? Before or after you slept with me?"

"I was never going to sleep with you. I only went along with it to buy time while I figured out a way to save my club."

"Go on with that lie Mateo. Had your employee not stopped us that night, we both know we wouldn't have stopped ourselves. You make me sick." I walk off.

"Lynn wait, please."

He catches up to me.

"What?"

"You and your husband need to be careful because Mattie will stop at nothing to get what she wants."

"Well, I will stop at nothing to make sure she doesn't."

Walking back to the locker room, I am fuming mad. I throw my towel and water bottle down on the bench before calling Jerome but he doesn't answer. I send him a text.

ME: Call me as soon as you get this message!

I fumble with the lock on my locker to get my gym bag. Snatching it out, I stop because I start to feel dizzy. I take a few breaths.

Then flashes of Jerome and Mattie begin filling my head.

"Not today devil." I say closing my eyes and laying my head against the locker.

"You okay?" A lady asks walking in.

"I'm fine. Thanks."

I take the things I need to shower because I have to get my car from the shop before they close at five and talking to Mateo put me behind. My car wouldn't start this morning so Jerome had it towed to the dealership and I am driving one of their courtesy cars.

Lilly, Mallory and Nathaniel went to Nashville Shores with some friends, to hang out before school starts and it has been a welcomed distraction.

Forty-five minutes later, I walk out the gym and as soon as I step out, the sky decides to open and rain, cats and dogs. Running to the car and rummaging for the key to this car, I drop my phone and the screen completely shatters.

"Great! Freaking great!" I scream! "WHAT ELSE GOD!"

The Marriage Bed

Mattie

"Where in the hell have you been?" Erica asks opening the door.

"Girl, it's only been a few days."

"Since I called you about that detective. He came back yesterday."

"So." I shrug.

"Mattie, this is serious. He's talking about there being an order of protection, against you for stalking." She yells.

"I'm not stalking anybody."

"Then why have you been ignoring me?"

"Hello!" I snap. "I was mad at you."

"Really Mattie? Are you still mad about me being pregnant when you were the one who hooked me up with Raymond, in the first place?"

"Yea, to get him off Jerome's back. You were supposed to keep him company, not get pregnant and catch feelings."

"Well, we both know plans change." She says plopping down on the couch.

"Anyway, I took your advice and I'm leaving Jerome alone."

She looks at me.

"I'm serious. I see that he isn't going to leave his wife for me and I'm not about to be one of those women on an episode of Snapped so I'm done."

"I don't believe you but okay."

"Damn E, what else do you want from me? You tell me to leave him alone and I did and you're still giving me hell about it."

"I know you Mattie and I also know how you can get." She says.

"That was the old me. Besides, he'll come to me sooner than later."

"What is that supposed to mean?" Erica questions and I shrug.

"Madeline Mattie Perez!" She yells my entire name. "What do you have planned?"

"Nothing." I tell her.

"Please don't do anything stupid for this man Mattie when you know he isn't going to leave his wife for you. And especially since you haven't even been honest about who you are. Does he know Mateo is your brother or even your real name?"

"That can be easily fixed with a conversation."

"What about the fact you can't really have children when you had him thinking you were pregnant before?"

"Minor issue." I say waving her off. "Anyway, enough about that, what do you have to drink?" I say not waiting for her to respond and walking into the kitchen. "You want something?"

"You are a piece of work but yea, bring me some tea."

I fix two glasses and join her in the living room. I sit on the end of the couch and put her feet in my lap.

She drinks most of the tea before putting the glass on the floor.

"Everything is going to work out E, you'll see."

"I hope so, for his sake."

Twenty-two minutes later, she is finally asleep.

"Damn!" I say pushing her legs off. "I thought that Melatonin would never kick in."

I get up and leave out the back door of her house, cutting through her back yard and walking two blocks over to this old SUV I purchased a few weeks back from Jackson, MS.

I get inside, buckle my seatbelt and start the truck before pulling out the piece of paper containing my list. "Now, let's find you."

I go to the house and park on the side of the street. I pull the hood over my head and walk up to the front door.

Ringing the doorbell, I put my hand into my pocket, just in case someone opens the door.

No answer.

I ring again.

"She's not here."

Getting back in the car, I drive through the parking lot of the Desoto Athletic Club.

I don't see her car and I get ready to pull off but I text Mateo.

ME: Hey, are you at the gym?

HIM: Nope, home. What's up?

ME: Nothing. Talk later.

Nope, she's not here either.

I pick up my list and scratch it off.

For the next thirty minutes, I drive by the parents' house and the church.

It starts to rain, with thunder and lightning but I only have one more place to check.

I pull in and do a quick scan.

"There you are. Come on girl and let's get this over with because I don't have all day." I say to myself.

I dial Erica's number and she doesn't answer which means she is still asleep.

"Finally." I say when I see her walking out. The umbrella is huge, but I know that walk.

Leaving a few seconds gap, I follow her out of the parking lot. I wait until we're on the two lane stretch of road, not far from the job that doesn't have a lot of traffic.

Taking in a deep breath, I punch the gas and ram the back of the car. My head flies forward and hits the steering wheel. I slam on brakes and she does the same. I blink a few times to get my focus but then I see the driver's side door open, her umbrella comes out and then her legs.

"Shit!" I say tapping on the steering wheel.

She starts walking towards the truck, so I punch the gas and run her over, sending her flying into the air. I look at the rearview, in enough time, to see her body hit the ground.

I drive to the outskirts of Memphis, to some part of Arkansas where I'd parked my car earlier. It's an area with overgrown and abandoned fields, I'd found on my hunt for a place to burn this truck.

I quickly park the truck in the middle of the field, grab a gas can from my trunk, douse it and use a book of matches to set it on fire. I undress and throw my clothes into the fire before taking another bag from the backseat that has a matching set of what I had on. I get dressed and head back.

Parking on the side of the street, I let the mirror down to check my face.

"Crap!" I scream when I see the gash on my forehead. I take some napkins from the door and an old bottle of water to wet them before wiping my head. I try to put my hair down over it to keep Erica from noticing. Getting out, I reach Erica's door and stop to see if I hear anything. Slowly opening it, she's still on the couch. I look at my watch and realize it's been almost three hours. She should be up by now.

I walk over and touch her.

"Erica?" Frantically shaking her. "Erica?"

"Hmm," she stirs. "What?"

"Oh, thank God!"

I sit back where I was and catch my breath. After a few minutes, I pull out my phone and send Jerome a text from the message app.

Little boo Jerome where is thy wife? Is she hard to find?

Have all the things that could go wrong started playing over in thy mind?

Maybe you should call or is she not answering the phone?

Well, may I suggest you try the morgue because your wife isn't coming home.

Jerome

"Mr. Watson, Sydney Gable is here."

I walk up to meet her.

"Sydney, it looks like you bought the storm with you."

"I know and it's coming down too." She says shaking out her umbrella.

"Reanna will show you to the design center." I tell her, motioning for Reanna. "I have the estimates and mock-ups drawn up and from there you can decide the direction you want to go in budget wise."

"Sounds great." She says.

"I will meet you all in there."

I walk into my office and grab my iPad and join them. We spend the next hour going over everything and making final decisions. Finally settled on all the designs and a starting date for renovations, I walk Sydney up front. She is our last client and Reanna is leaving early for a doctor's appointment.

"Mr. Watson, do you need anything before I go?" Reanna asks.

"No, everything is taken care of, for the most part. I only have a few contracts to finalize and emails to reply too. Are you going to be okay getting to your car in this rain? I don't need you falling."

"Yes, my husband is outside. You know he is not going to miss a doctor's appointment." She says rubbing her growing stomach.

"I cannot blame him. Having a family is the most precious thing."

I wait for her to grab her computer bag and purse in order to hold the door while she opens her umbrella. I wave at her husband, who meets her.

Since I'm not expecting anyone else, I lock the door.

Making it to my desk, I pick up my phone and see a text from Lynn from over an hour ago.

LYNN: Call me as soon as you get this message!

I dial her number but she doesn't answer. I call her again, still no answer.

I send her a text.

ME: Hey, I am just seeing your text. Call me.

I put the phone on the desk and I get a feeling in the pit of my stomach. I go over to the couch and kneel beside it.

"God, I know I made a mess of things and due to my selfish ways I have put my family in danger. I bought this attack on my family because I was out of your will and I'm sorry. Please forgive me for ever thinking I could get away sleeping with sin. All I ask is for you to cover and protect my family and all those connected to me because they didn't ask for this. Please sir. Amen."

I stay there a minute longer before going into the bathroom. I come out and walk into the design center to get the mockups for Sydney's project and a few others. I make it back to my desk and begin to work.

I get caught up in finalizing contracts and responding to emails that I lose track of time. I pick up my phone to see it's after five.

I call Lynn again.

No answer.

I wait a few minutes, trying not to panic.

I call again.

Still no answer.

I lay it down and pace the office. I go back to my phone and see a text in the unknown senders' box from about thirty minutes ago. I click on it.

Little boo Jerome where is thy wife? Is she hard to find?

Have all the things that could go wrong started playing over in thy mind?

Maybe you should call or is she not answering the phone?

Well, may I suggest you try the morgue because your wife isn't coming home.

I hear knocking on the door. I get up and when I turn the corner, I see Marcus. I quickly open it.

"Marcus, what's wrong?"

"Jerome, you need to come with me."

"What's going on?"

"Jerome, I need you to come with me."

"Sure, but am I in some sort of trouble?"

"No but's about your wife." He somberly states. "Get your things and I'll explain."

"Is she okay? I've been calling her, the past hour. Did something happen?"

He looks down.

"Marcus, just tell me."

"Jerome, there's been an accident. Get your things and come with me."

With the sirens blaring, Marcus or Detective Gaiters speeds out of the parking lot. My phone vibrates in my pocket from an unknown number, I press decline.

"Marcus, tell me what happened."

"There was an accident about an hour and half ago, on the back road behind your building. It was a hit and run and the woman did not survive. I'm sorry but--"

"Was it Lynn?"

"I cannot give you a positive identification."

"Marcus, is it Lynn? Please just tell me? Is it my wife?"

He doesn't say anything.

I scream hitting the dashboard.

"Damn it! All of this is my fault. This is all my fault."

We pull into Regional One's Ambulance Bay in less than fifteen minutes. He doesn't say anything as I follow him into the hospital. He stops to speak to a nurse who points us in the direction of some double doors.

Walking, my heart is beating at what feels like, a thousand beats per minute.

I watch Marcus stop and talk to another man who looks over at me. The man then walks over and whispers something into my ear.

I look at him before looking at Marcus.

He says something else before walking off.

"Jerome." Marcus says pulling me out of my thoughts.

"Before I open this door, I need you to understand the severity of what you are about to see. The truck hit her, knocking her into the air before her body hit the ground. I can understand if you don't want to see her, right now."

"I need to. It's my fault she's here. Please let me see her." He pushes the door open to a room and I stop in the door when I see her lying in the bed with a sheet up to her neck.

I walk over and stand there.

"I'm so sorry." I cry. "I'm so sorry!"

BREAKING NEWS AT FIVE

"Police are on the scene of a deadly hit-and-run in the 9000 block of Holmes Road. Police say a female, who has not been identified, was hit after getting out of her car during what look to have started out as an ordinary accident. The hit-and-run happened this afternoon around 3:30pm. A witness told police the car was hit from behind, by a black SUV. When the driver of the car got out, the driver of the SUV deliberately ran her over.

All we know, at the moment, is the first car is a 2017 Lexus with TN tags and the second, is a truck being driven by an African American female. It did not have a license plate. Police say the truck will have major front-end damage but please do not try to approach it. If you see the truck or if you have any information that can help investigators, please call crime stoppers at the number listed on your screen.

This is Sean Chapman reporting live from the scene. We will bring you more on this breaking news story tonight at 10."

Mattie

"Police say the truck will have major front-end damage but please do not try to approach it. If you see the truck or if you have any information that can help investigators, please call crime stoppers at the number listed on your screen. This is Sean Chapman reporting live from the scene. We will bring you more on this breaking news story tonight at 10."

Erica turns off the TV.

"Man, that's awful. You hungry?" I ask her.

"Mattie," Erica says looking at me with tears in her eyes, "please tell me this has nothing to do with you."

"What are you talking about?" I ask her.

"Did you kill that lady?"

"Girl, you don't even know who the lady is. They just said she is unidentified. Besides, why would you automatically assume I had anything to do with an accident after hearing this story? You think I did that drive by in North Memphis too?"

"Where is the truck you bought a few weeks back?"

"It's at home in my garage."

"I don't believe you." She says getting up. When she does, she staggers.

"Whoa, you okay?"

"No, I feel dizzy."

"Sit down. Have you eaten?" I ask as she reaches for the glass she has by the couch.

I snatch it from her hand.

"I'll get you some more tea." I say walking into the living room.

When I come back, she is leaned over with her head in her hands.

"You okay?" I sit beside her.

"Yea, probably just morning sickness." She replies.

"I'll let you go so you can lay down."

"No! You're going to tell me what you did because we both know it's no coincidence that a 2017 Lexus in the 9000 block of Holmes was involved in an accident. Come on Mattie, we both know what that adds up too."

"No, we don't." I tell her. "You know how many people drive a 2017 Lexus in Memphis in the 9000 block of Holmes?"

"No, I only know one and she happens to be married to the man you're having an affair with. And that road, is a back street that not a lot of people use. You only know about it because Jerome told you and you have a gash on your forehead so, for the last time, what did you do?"

I start picking at my nails.

"Mattie, what did you do?" She yells.

"What I had too." I answer. "But don't worry, it can't be traced back to me."

"Are you stupid? Who else had a motive to murder her?" She cries. "Oh my God Mattie, what have you done? You know you will not survive in jail."

"Girl stop crying because I'm not going to jail. Anyway, how long do you think it'll take for them to notify Jerome?"

"Are you for real, right now? That should be the least of your worries. How can you be so freaking nonchalant about this?" She asks.

"Look, I got to go. I need to shower, change clothes and do my hair because Jerome will need me to console him when he finds out."

I walk to the door but then I turn back to Erica.

"I can trust you to stay quiet right?"

She's crying and shaking her head, yes.

"Good because I'd hate for something terrible to happen to you too."

I get to the car and pull out my phone. I refresh my Safari page that's open to Channel 3 News to see if there's been an update.

None.

I call Jerome but hang up.

I open my message app to text him but I lock the phone and throw it onto the passenger seat.

"He'll call."

Jerome

Four Days Later

I walk into Harrison Memorial Chapel with Lilly, Nathaniel, Mallory, Frank and Wanda for the private viewing.

We see the stand, outside the chapel door that has her picture next to it on an easel.

I grab Mallory's hand while Lilly and Nathaniel walk behind us.

I take a deep breath.

I asked Pastor and Lady Carrington and Deacon Raymond Matthews and his wife to be here with us.

Star, who works for the funeral home closes the door behind us.

After about thirty minutes, my phone vibrates.

"Lilly, I'll be right back. Stay with your brother and sister."

I walk out to see Mattie standing there, holding one black rose.

"What in the hell are you doing here?" I ask grabbing her arm and pulling her to the side.

"I only came to check on you and offer my support seeing you've been MIA. Where have you been? It's been almost a week." She states snatching her arm away. "You been staying with another bitch?"

"Are you crazy? Mattie, I've been mourning with my children because someone took their mother away from them." I tell her.

"I know and that's even more reason you should have called me. I need to be here for you."

"No, you need to go." I say looking around.

"Baby, where have you been staying?" She whines rubbing my arm. "I've been worried sick. I went by the house and the flowers I sent are still on the porch. You haven't been to Lynn's parents' house either."

"You've been watching me?"

"Yes, because I know you're seeing somebody else! You dirty--," she looks around before inhaling and exhaling. "Baby, you need to let me be here for you because I would hate for something else to happen."

"You need to leave."

She takes a step back. "Jerome, Lynn was my friend and I have every right to be here."

"How did you even know about this visitation? It's private and hasn't been posted anywhere."

"That doesn't matter baby, I'm only here to make sure you're okay?"

I put my back against the wall.

"You cannot go in there because everybody will know."

"I'm just a friend and church member who is coming to pay her respects." She says smoothing her dress. "That's all I am. Today."

"Mattie, please don't go in there." I beg.

"It'll be okay."

I watch her go over to the doors where she stops to look at the picture and then back at me with a smile before walking in. A few seconds later, I go in behind her.

Heading towards the casket with all eyes on her, it's like she's loving the attention. When she gets to the casket, she gasps, dropping the rose she was holding before looking back at me. I motion for Frank and Wanda to take the children out.

"What's going on?" She asks looking around. "There is no body. Where is the body Jerome?"

"What body?"

"WHERE.IS.SHE?"

"Where is who?"

"Your wife!" She screams.

"I'm right here?" Lynn answers walking in with Detective Gaiters behind her.

"What the fu—wait," she turns, bumping into the casket causing it to rock. "Jerome, what is going on?"

"The lady you murdered was Sydney Gable, the newly elected youth pastor of the church. A woman who had nothing, at all, to do with this. A woman, in the prime of her life, who was preparing to renovate the home she was hoping to share with her husband who is deployed overseas. Instead he has to come home to bury her. Her parents are devastated because when they should be flying to Memphis to hear her first sermon, it'll be to claim her body."

"Why are you telling this?" She passively asks. "I had nothing to do with what happened to her. I'm leaving."

The doors open and everybody turns around to see Erica walk in.

"No boo, the only place you're going is jail." Lynn says.

"Look, I don't know what that bitch told you," She yells pointing at Erica, "but she's lying. She's nothing more than a common whore who is pregnant by Deacon Matthews. I bet y'all didn't know that, did you?"

Nobody says anything.

"They know." Erica says. "I told them everything and I asked for forgiveness. What about you Madeline Perez? You care to confess?"

"I have nothing to confess. I want a lawyer."

"We have all the evidence we need anyway." Marcus says walking up to Mattie. "Turn around. Madeline Perez or Mattie Green, you have the right to remain silent. Anything you say can and will be used against you in a court of law. You have the right to have an attorney. If you cannot afford one, one will be appointed to you by the court. Do you understand these rights?"

"What if I say no?" She laughs.

"Ma'am, you can take this as a joke, but it isn't. You took a woman's life."

"You can't prove anything. LAWYER!" Mattie screams in his face.

"Isn't it amazing what cameras show, nowadays?" Lynn asks looking at me.

"Yes, technology is quite amazing." I reply. "Due to some recent break-ins of businesses around the area, I got together with some of the companies and we installed a security system covering every area of the corporate park. It just so happened to catch you, Mattie, on the lot that day."

"That means nothing. I've been to your place of employment many times, remember?" She smiles.

"Yea but an employee of Pfizer, which happens to sit behind Watson Construction, got into an argument with his wife who put him out the car, on the very stretch of road where the accident happened. Care to guess what he witnessed?" Marcus asks.

"Everybody seemed to have been where they should have except the person I wanted." Mattie says glaring at Lynn.

"Well, mistress boo, had you kept up with me like you tried, you would have known my car was in the shop that day. However, you were so hell bent on getting rid of me that you never even stopped to notice, it wasn't my car or me. All you saw was what hatred and jealousy allowed you to see and it took an innocent woman's life. I pray God has mercy on your filthy soul." Lynn tells her.

"Keep your funky prayers!" Mattie barks. "Forget all of y'all. You can stand here, judging me with your Christian talk all you want but I am not the only one who must atone for this sin. Every one of you are just as guilty as I am. The only difference, my sin has been brought to light but be careful because while it's me today, it could be your turn tomorrow."

"You're right Mattie, none of us are perfect. I made a mistake and it cost this woman her life." I say pointing to the empty casket. "That's something I will have to live with for the rest of my life but I will not allow you to guilt me into taking on your burden. Yes, I hurt my family and I will work on gaining their forgiveness and their trust but you, you did this."

"SO WHAT?" She screams. "I never would have done this had you kept your promises. You said you loved me and you promised me the world then expected me to be happy with a snow globe and a pat on the head. You didn't get to decide when it was over. You didn't get to play with my emotions and then go back home to your family."

"Why go after my wife when this had nothing to do with her? You could have taken it out on me."

"No, no, no;" She says smiling and shaking her head. "If I couldn't be happy, neither could you. If I had to sleep in a lonely bed at night, so should you."

"What about our children?" Lynn asks.

She rolls her eyes and turns to Marcus. "Can we go now because I'm getting bored? Oh, and for the record, I knew it was Sydney when I saw her get out the truck."

"Then why kill her?" Marcus asks her.

"Because Jerome was screwing her too."

Marcus walks her out, I turn to those in the room.

"Lynn baby, she's lying." I say walking towards her. "You have to believe me. I was not sleeping with Sydney."

"Now seems like a great moment to pause in prayer." Pastor Carrington cuts in.

I get Wanda, Frank and the children and we all stand around holding hands.

"Our heavenly father, we come petitioning your throne today first to say thank you. Thank you for your many blessings, your covering, your protection and your provision. God, as we stand in the midst of this chapel, we pause here and ask you to bless the family of Sydney Gable whose life was taken from us prematurely. We don't always understand but we trust you. And God, for those of us left behind, heal us. Heal us from the hurt and pain but most importantly, forgive us. Forgive us for the mistakes we've made, for the wayward thinking and our actions. Forgive us for thinking we could prosper outside of your will and forgive for trying to handle things on our own. Cleanse us, from the inside out and reconcile hearts. Bless God and mend what man has broken and restore what sin has destroyed for we know you have the power. And God, bless the new lives that have been conceived during this troublesome time and we pray their arrivals will return the joy and light, pushing out darkness. Bless and forgive Mattie, God for she is your child. This prayer we offer in your son Jesus name, amen."

We all say amen before Lynn storms out.

Lynn

Five Days Prior

I open my eyes to see an unknown lady standing over me.

"Ma'am, please lay still." She requests.

"Huh?" I ask looking around. "What are you doing?"

She looks at something in her hand. "Mrs. Watson, you passed out in the parking lot of the gym and someone called 911. My name is Ashley and I am an EMT, here to help. Do you understand?"

My face must show my confusion.

"Were you feeling ill or having pain anywhere?"

"I felt a little dizzy after my workout but nothing major." I reply. "I'm cold."

"You are wet from the rain but we have plenty of blankets on you. Have you eaten today?" She asks writing something on a clipboard.

"Yes, well I had a smoothie and banana for breakfast but nothing since."

"Do you have a history of heart disease, high blood pressure or passing out?"

I shake my head no.

"Is there a chance you could be pregnant?"

"No." I tell her closing my eyes. "I need to call my husband."

"We will have someone contact him as soon as we get to the hospital." She says. "Can you tell me what hospital you would like to be taken too."

"Do I really have to be taken? I feel fine."

"It is totally up to you, but you did lose consciousness and you should get checked out."

"I will let you take me if I can call my husband and any Methodist Hospital is fine." I barter.

She finally pulls a phone from her pocket and hands it to me.

I dial Jerome's cell phone number but he doesn't answer.

I hand her the phone back.

"We will make sure someone contacts him." She says.

It's been over three hours but I am finally settled into a room in the emergency department of Methodist Hospital. I haven't had a chance to ask the nurse if she was able to get in touch with Jerome because I've been sent for test after test while doctors and nurses have been in and out.

Closing my eyes, I hear the door open. Jerome comes rushing to the bed.

"Jerome, where have you been?" I ask when he buries his head in my chest.

"I thought you were dead."

"What? Why would you think that?"

He continues to hold me while he cries. I don't say anything.

When he's done, he stands up.

"Sydney Gable is dead."

"How?"

"A hit-and-run." He says pulling a chair to the bed.

"What aren't you telling me?"

He pulls his phone from his pocket and hands it to me.

"Wow! Did she--"

He grabs my hand. "Lynn, I am so sorry. All of this is because of me. I don't know what I would have done had something happened to you. What would I have told the children? I'm so sorry."

He lays his head on the bed and begins to cry again.

I rub my hand over his head while I give him time to get it out.

"You're right, this is your fault but there is nothing we can do about what you've done. You cheated, and you have to live with it and as much as I want to make you suffer for it, I can't because I have no power to be judge or executioner over your life. What I can do, at this moment, is decide what I want going forward and I don't know if that includes you."

He gets ready to speak but there is a knock on the door.

"Mrs. Watson how are you feeling?"

"I am feeling fine doctor and I hope that will remain the same once you are done with the results of my tests." I say smiling.

"Well that will depend on how you handle what I'm about to tell you."

"Okay?"

"You're pregnant." He says.

I laugh.

"You're kidding, right? What are the real results, dehydration or something?"

"From your bloodwork, you look to be about six to eight weeks along coupled with a little dehydration, resulting in dizziness and fainting. All the remaining tests were negative. I want you to finish that bag of fluids and we will get you out of here with orders to see your OBGYN. Do you have any questions for me?"

"Yes. What are my options for terminating?"

Jerome

While waiting on Lynn's discharge papers, my phone vibrates with a call from Marcus.

"Hey Marcus, is everything okay?" I ask putting the phone on speaker.

"How's Lynn?"

"She's good, we are waiting for her discharge papers." I reply.

"That's great news, especially after everything that has happened tonight." He sighs. "Speaking of, have you had a chance to talk to Lynn about what we discussed?"

She looks at me, confused just as the nurse knocks on the door.

"No, I haven't had an opportunity but I will as soon as we get out of here."

"Are you all going to the safe house?"

"Yes."

"Cool, I will meet you there." Marcus says hanging up.

"Okay Mrs. Watson, here is your paperwork." The nurse says walking in. "As the doctor stated, follow up with your OBGYN and he or she can answer any questions you have related to options for this pregnancy. As of now, are there any questions I can answer for you?"

"None that can't wait for my doctor but thank you." Lynn replies taking the paperwork from the nurse.

"Would you like a wheelchair? It's customary for us to bring one but it is totally up to you."

"No, I'm good to walk." I tell her.

"Then you all have a great rest of your night."

I try to help Lynn get dressed but she waves me off.

"Are you seriously thinking about terminating this pregnancy?" I ask.

"Are you seriously thinking about keeping it? Jerome look at where we are."

"We can fix us." I state.

"No boo, there is no fixing this."

"Lynn, I am not perfect. I made a mistake and it is one I will spend the rest of my life trying to make up for it."

She sits on the side of the bed. "Jerome, cut the bull. You are no sorrier than you were the first time. If you would, you would stop cheating."

"I have."

She laughs. "You really do take me for a fool. Dude take me home before you need stitches."

We pull up to a house. I reach into the console of the car for the key fob to open the gate. Getting inside, Lynn goes to look around. She walks into the kitchen and begins opening cabinets.

"Until you explain what we're doing here and whose car that is, can I at least make some hot tea?"

"Yes, you can use whatever you want but I can do that for you while you relax."

"Jerome, I'm capable of making a cup of tea."

"I'm only trying to help."

"STOP!" She says throwing the cup into the sink, breaking it into pieces. "Did you argue with me on my birthday just so I'd leave the house?"

"Of course not, why would you think that?"

She turns to me and has tears streaming down her face.

"Mateo is Mattie's brother and she sent him to seduce me, hoping if I cheated on you, you'd leave me for her. He was the one taking pictures of me at the club. I guess Mattie is the one who sent them to Deacon Matthews."

"I, wait, I didn't know. I promise I didn't know." I walk near her but she puts up her hand, shaking her head.

"Let me hold you baby. I know I hurt you but can't I at least console you?"

"No." She says wiping her face. "You don't get to console me when you were the one who caused my tears. As a matter of fact, don't even come close to me because I don't want to give in seeing you were once my comfortable place."

"Is you giving in to me a bad thing?" I ask her.

"Jerome, your arms used to make me feel safe and laying my head on your chest use to give me peace. Being with you and our children, at our home, used to be my piece of paradise because I knew if I made it home, nothing out in the world could hurt me. It's tainted now. Yes, you used to be my comfortable place but now its community property and has lost its value."

"Baby, please don't give up on us. God is giving us another chance, with a new life growing inside of you."

The doorbell rings.

"Who says it's yours?" She asks as the doorbell sounds again.

I open my mouth to say something, but I don't and instead walk away. She follows me to the front door, where I open the door for Marcus.

"You remember Marcus, well he's Detective Marcus Gaiters now with Memphis Police."

"Of course I do." She says giving him a hug. "How have you been?"

"I've been great? Keeping busy with the crime rate in Memphis. I hope you all are finding what you need in the house."

"Everything except why we're here." Lynn says.

"I will explain." He says.

We all go into the living room and take a seat.

"I don't know how much Jerome has told you but there was an accident involving a 2017 Lexus, not far from Jerome's office. The driver of the car was Sydney Gable. Unfortunately, she did not survive." Marcus says pulling a notepad from his pocket.

"He told me that much." Lynn says.

"Jerome and I met earlier in the day, at his office and he told me about Mattie. I was in the middle of digging up some information on her when I heard the call about the accident. I went to the scene because the description of the car and victim was so similar to you Lynn, even down to your natural hair." He tells her.

"Wait, hold on. There seems to be some pieces missing." Lynn says. "Why were you at Jerome's office?"

"I've been receiving calls and texts from Mattie nonstop since I told you about the affair. She sent me an email that I took as a threat so just to be safe, I called Marcus for advice."

"And you didn't think to tell me?"

"I wanted to know my options before I told you everything." I say.

"What other secrets are you holding?"

"Lynn, it's not like that." I sigh. "Sydney was at my office finalizing plans for renovations we were supposed to start at her house next week. I guess the accident happened soon after she left."

"Yeah. There was a witness walking in the area, who saw the entire thing."

"Okay but why are we here now? Can't you all go and arrest her?"

"We don't know where she is. The address we have on file is a friend's house. Therefore, we need your help to draw her out."

"What can I do?" Lynn asks.

"We want to fake your death." Marcus says.

Lynn

"Do what now?"

"It sounds like a crazy idea Lynn, but Mattie has gone through a lot of trouble to cover her tracks. The truck used was found burnt to the metal in a rural of Arkansas and we're having trouble even finding evidence that she purchased it." Marcus says.

"Then how do you know it was her?"

"A statement given by an Erica Gomez."

"Erica turned her in?" I ask.

"Yes, and without her statement, we'd only have the video of her on the parking lot and a description of a truck but nothing else. Anyway, the quicker we can get her off the street, the better I'd feel knowing she will not have the chance to hurt you or your family again." Marcus clarifies.

"So, what do you have in mind?"

"We will set up a private visitation, just for family and leak it to her and see if she bites." Jerome says.

"If she doesn't?"

"Then we will try something else." He says.

"What about my children and parents? I will not have them believing I'm dead."

"I wouldn't ask you too but we have to be careful, in case she's watching. That's why I didn't want you all to go back to your house. I will go and speak to your parents and make it as if they are being notified. Jerome is going to talk to your pastor to get him involved and we've already spoken to Erica."

"And the children?"

"They will be back tomorrow afternoon. I'll get them and explain." Jerome states.

"How soon will we do this?" I ask.

"Three to five days, at least."

"Fine but it better work or I will find her myself."

Arraignment

"All rise. The court is now in session, honorable Judge Tabitha Emerson presiding. Please be seated."

"Good morning, we are here for the arraignment of Madeline Lucia Perez." The judge states. "Will the lawyers please state your name for the record?"

"Good morning your honor, Tom Dyer on behalf of the state of Tennessee."

"Sherry Garry for the state of Tennessee."

"And Randall Ewing on behalf of Ms. Perez."

"Ms. Perez, you have been charged by indictment, in count one with Homicide, murder in the 1st Degree with pre-meditation of Sydney Gable on Thursday, July 19, 2018. This is a First-Degree felony, punishable by up to death. The state has filed its notice of their intent to seek life in prison without parole. Count two of --"

"Your honor, we wave formal reading of the indictment at this time. We have been provided copies of these indictments by the state of Tennessee and have reviewed them with Ms. Perez. She is aware of the charges she's facing." Mr. Ewing states.

"The only other issue is how your defendant will stand."

"In terms of entering a plea, we stand mute, your honor." Attorney Ewing answers.

"Any objection to the mute and formal reading?" Judge Emerson asks.

"No, your honor."

"Since you are waiving formal reading and are standing mute, pursuant to rule 3.170C, a plea of Not Guilty shall be entered on the defendant's behalf on all counts of the indictment. I'll set trial date for November 13, 2018. Does that work for everybody?"

"Yes, your honor." They state.

"What is the people on bail?" Judge asks.

"Your honor, we ask the defendant be held without bond. She deliberately ran Ms. Gable over after ramming the back of her car. We have evidence of her threats to the husband of her intended victim and we feel she is a violent and dangerous threat to society." Attorney Garry states.

"Your honor, my client has no previous criminal record, she has ties to the community and she owns a popular nightclub with her brother. She knows the seriousness of what she has been charged with and we have no doubt she will return for trial. Your honor, she is not a danger to society, just a victim of domestic abuse by a man she thought loved her that caused her actions." Attorney Ewing declares.

"Saved your theories for trial counselor. Looking at the case I have before me, the allegations and the seriousness of this crime; I am incline to agree with the people and I find it appropriate to have Ms. Perez held without bond."

The courtroom is filled with sobs from Erica who is being consoled by Mateo. I look over at Lynn who has her eyes closed and then at Mattie who shows no type of emotion. Her attorney whispers something in her ear and she shrugs.

"We stand adjourn. Ms. Perez, you are now in the officers' custody."

When the officers grab her arm to walk her out, she looks back at me and smile, mouthing the words, I love you.

Lynn chuckles before grabbing her purse. "Aw how sweet, she loves you." She says before brushing by me.

ONE WEEK LATER

Restoration Session

Lynn

"Hi, my name is Dr. Mitchell and you must be Jerome and Lynn Watson."

"Yes." We both say at the same time.

"Great, come in. Can I offer either of you some water?" She asks.

We shake our heads no.

"Before you take your seat, I like to open and end with prayer, is that okay with both of you?"

We shake our heads yes and grab hands.

"Dear God, we come this afternoon thanking you for another day. God, as we gather here, I ask you for your presence to encamp here because we know where you are, your grace abounds. Bless this gathering of restoration that our minds may be open to receive what is needed to repair what has been broken. Amen."

Jerome and I both say amen.

She grabs her iPad and sits in her chair while we sit across from her on the couch.

"As I stated, my name is Dr. Savannah Mitchell. I do not refer to our meetings as therapy, but I like to call them restoration sessions because it is my hope, once we are done, both of you will leave here restored in some way. Now, tell me what's broken." She requests.

"Our marriage because I had an affair," Jerome states.

"Was it the first time?"

"Yes." He replies.

"How long ago did the affair end? Dr. Mitchell asks.

I look at Jerome, waiting for the answer but he doesn't say anything.

"Dr. Mitchell, you may need to clarify which affair because apparently he's had more than one."

"That's not true." Jerome clarifies. "There has been only one."

"You don't have to lie anymore boo, our marriage is over." I tell him.

"Then why are we here?" He yells.

"You made the appointment remember?"

"Lynn why are you so angry?" Dr. Mitchell inquires.

"What else am I supposed to feel? This man, my husband of eighteen years cheated but wait because that's not the worse part. Oh no, the worse and most hurtful part of all this, it was with someone we knew. A lady we worshipped with every Sunday and fellowshipped with at church functions. They both stood in my face knowing they were lying to me. Angry is all I got doc because it's either anger, aggravated assault or murder."

"I made a mistake." Jerome says.

"A mistake is picking up the wrong kind of milk. A mistake is putting sugar instead of salt. A mistake is two different color socks. Having an affair isn't a mistake, it's a choice. A choice you made every time you met Mattie for sex, sent naked pictures, told her you loved her, talked about getting rid of me and letting her in our bed. Those are choices, sweetheart. Choices you made when you decided to be with her and God only knows who else."

"It was one freaking mistake!" Jerome yells.

"One freaking mistake." I repeat after standing up. "Well Jerome, one mistake can cost you your business, a lot of money or even your life; on a construction site. One mistake for Dr. Mitchell can cost her medical license. One mistake for me, behind the wheel of my car, can paralyze a person. We discipline our children for one mistake. We take away privileges for one mistake. One mistake is, sometimes, all it takes. I'm sorry Dr. Mitchell but I need some air."

Jerome

Dr. Mitchell gets up and follows Lynn out. A few minutes later, she returns without her.

I stand up. "Is she okay?"

"She's hurt."

"Do I need to check on her?"

"No, let's give her some time to herself while we talk. Is that alright with you?"

"Sure." I take my seat.

"Why did you get married?"

I smile thinking back to when I first saw Lynn. "I met Lynn in the halls of Booker T. Washington High School back in 1993. She was vibrant and caring and looked at me like there was nobody else in the room. When my mom walked out, during my senior year, leaving me with my abusive father; she was there. She stuck with me when I struggled in school and almost flunked out of college. She stayed, the many times I pushed her away because of the pain inflicted by my father. Dr. Mitchell, I had to marry her because she made me better. She grew me up and didn't allow me to follow in the footsteps, generational curses created."

We turn when we hear clapping.

"Wow Jerome." Lynn says wiping her eyes. "And the award, ladies and gentlemen."

"Lynn are you rejoining us?" Dr. Mitchell asks.

"Sure, because I've got to hear what else my husband has to lie about."

"Babe, I am sorry for hurting you and I never set out to break your heart." I say, turning to her.

"But you didn't just break my heart Jerome," she pauses, "you also broke me."

"How Lynn? Explain to Jerome how his infidelity broke you." Dr. Mitchell instructs.

"Why? It's not like it matters anymore because if I mattered to my husband, he never would have done this."

"My cheating had nothing to do with you Lynn. I cheated because I got comfortable, complacent and careless not because I wanted to break you or your heart. I was stupid. Plain and simple!"

"Tell her what you mean." Dr. Mitchell states. "You cannot just leave it there because she needs to know."

I exhale. "Lynn, you have been my only partner, in everything, since we were seventeen and I got so comfortable with what we'd created I thought as long as I continued to do what you and the children needed, provided for our household and showed up for the things you required, it would be enough. You were good to me and I became complacent or unconcerned about losing you. Again, I thought you'd always be there and that's why I was careless. Careless in being able to stand and look you in the eyes and lie."

"You got comfortable enough to become unworried and inconsiderate towards your family?" Lynn asks. "Do you really think that less of us?"

"No, I got comfortable enough not to worry because I was selfish. I'm sorry."

"STOP APOLOGIZING!" Lynn yells. "Apologizing doesn't pardon you from the circumstances you created. You sit here with this smug look on your face, pretending to be the apologetic husband but you're not. You wanting us to come to therapy isn't about fixing what YOU broke more than keeping the lifestyle. Well, it can't. Your comfort, complacency and carelessness destroyed everything our struggle paid for and I'm sorry cannot repair it. Not this time."

"Lynn, this isn't about keeping up a lifestyle, you have to believe that. I love you and I've seen what my mistakes have done to you and I never want you to feel the way you do now."

"Why did it have to take seeing me hurt instead of knowing I would be? Jerome, why was it so easy for you to throw away all we've built? You allowed quick moments of intimacy, with another woman and maybe more, to destroy everything we sacrificed for. Why?"

"I wasn't thinking about any of that babe. I don't mean to sound uncaring but those times I was sending texts, pictures and laying with another woman; I wasn't thinking about you, our children, home or business. It was all about my flesh being satisfied. I wasn't thinking about all we've built because during those times, it was as if I was an addict fulfilling my addiction." I tell her.

"Wow, I think that's probably one of the first honest things you've said about this entire situation." Lynn responds wiping tears. "Thank you. It doesn't change the course of this marriage, but I appreciate it."

"Why can't it? I made one mistake out of all the years we've been together, shouldn't that count for something?" I ask getting agitated.

"Yea, it counts for us being married this long. Jerome, you don't get points for honoring the vows and sanctity of marriage you entered in. Hell, this isn't high school where you get credit for doing what you are supposed to do. Marriage doesn't work like that and you know it."

"What else do you want from me? I'm sorry for being human and thinking I was strong enough to handle the temptations of my flesh. I am sorry for not being you Lynn."

She laughs.

"What's funny Lynn?" Dr. Mitchell questions.

"The fact this Negro is trying to place the blame on me. Do you know how many times I've wanted to give in to my flesh? Do you know the many times I've been hit on by men, who I could have turned too, while my husband was forsaking his marriage bed? Do you know the temptations I've had to overcome?"

"Like Mateo?" I cut in. "You did say it was a possibility the baby wasn't mine."

She looks at me. "Mane please! I only said that to get back at you because you know I have never cheated on you. It doesn't mean I haven't wanted too but--"

"Why do you always do that?" I ask, interrupting her.

"What is she doing Jerome?" Dr. Mitchell probes.

"Throwing in the 'I wanted to but' statements. She does it all the time and it's irritating."

"It's irritating?" She laughs. "Irritating is wanting your husband to touch you in places he's forgotten about instead you have to buy sex toys to make up for his lack. Irritating is lying awake, at night, horny with a husband next to you that refuses to satisfy you because he's "tired"." She mocks with air quotes. "Irritating is thinking there is something wrong with me when all along it's been you. That's irritating. And if it's irritating to hear how many times I've had the chance to cheat but DIDN'T so freaking what! Deal with it! I wasn't the one who didn't hold up our agreement."

"Okay, let's take a breath. Would either of you like some water?"

Lynn and I both say no.

After a few more seconds Dr. Mitchell breaks the silence. "What agreement are you referring to Lynn?"

"Tell her!" Lynn gestures getting up from the couch.

I sigh. "When we were first married, a mutual decision was made that if we ever felt the desire to explore, outside of the marriage, we'd talk about it because we didn't want our marriage bed defiled."

Lynn chuckles, "And look how that worked out."

"Jerome, if you knew you had this agreement why not talk to Lynn first?" Dr. Mitchell asks. "Why not avoid all the troubles an affair created when you have a wife willing to compromise for your wants?"

"Not just wants, Dr. Mitchell because I was open to his desires too." She states.

"Jerome?"

I run my hand over my face before sitting up. "I knew she'd allow it but then I'd probably have to be in agreement with her wanting the same thing in return and I couldn't do that."

"Oh, just so we're clear. You had an affair because if you asked for permission and I allowed it, you thought I'd want permission too and you can't fathom another man touching me? Is that correct husband?"

"Yea." I reply softly.

"I didn't hear you." Lynn says coming closer to me.

"YES!"

"Well, isn't that sweet. My husband was looking out for me." She says teases.

"Babe, that's my truth." I reply.

"Screw your truth! You were selfish!" She yells.

"Okay, how about we end this session, for now." Dr. Mitchell says.

"No, how about we end this marriage because I am done. It is obvious we've outgrown each other." Lynn says.

"Jerome," Dr. Mitchell says, "Do you feel this is true?"

"No and I'm sorry I have made her feel like this." I say again. "I made a mistake and I want to fix our marriage, but I don't know how. Lynn, I love you and I want our marriage."

"Are we done?" She asks in response.

I turn away.

"Yes," Dr. Mitchell says, "however I would like to see both of you again. I will leave it up to each of you to decide whether to continue together or separately. Whatever you decide, call my office to schedule the appointment. Let us pray."

"God, right now it is your servant seeking a moment of your time. God, you already know the desires of our heart because you created us and right now, I simply need you to guide. Guide this man and this woman into their rightful place. Your word says, let no man put asunder who you have joined but what if the season is over? God, we need clarity then understanding and finally strength for we know all things work for those who love you. We love you God, we trust you and we take nothing for granted but we'll give everything for grace because You can restore even if restoration must happen separately. We thank you

God and we humbly submit this prayer, awaiting your response. Amen."

Lynn

We walk out of Dr. Mitchell's office.

"I am sorry for everything Lynn." Jerome says to me when we make it to our vehicles.

"I know, and you don't have to keep apologizing. I'm over it."

"Really Lynn?"

"Yes, really Jerome."

He nods. "Can we at least have lunch to discuss the baby?"

"No, I have a doctor's appointment."

"Why didn't you tell me?" He says looking at his watch. "I have an hour before my next appointment so I can take you and bring you back to your car."

"I wasn't inviting you."

"Lynn--"

"Jerome, I haven't made a decision on whether I am keeping the baby. However, this is only a doctor's appointment and I'm going by myself. We will talk when I am ready too."

He sighs, I get in my car and pull off.

*****

"Hi, Dr. West."

"Hey Lynn, how are you?" She asks coming into the room.

"I'm good."

"It's good to see you. I don't think I've seen you this entire year, but I see from the chart you're pregnant." She smiles but then steps back. "Judging from your face, this wasn't planned."

"God no and I am not sure if I want to keep the baby, Dr. West." I burst into tears. "Does that make me a bad person?"

"Of course not, it makes you a woman with choices." She gives me a Kleenex before pulling her stool to the end of the table and sitting down. "What's going on with you? You've been my patient since you were pregnant with Lilly and I've never seen you this upset."

"There's been a lot of things going on in my personal life and a baby right now is bad timing. Plus, I had some drinks and I smoked a cigar, a few weeks ago. What if something is wrong with the baby?"

"I've seen the story on the news and although I've never been in your shoes I will tell you this, don't make a big decision while you're emotional. You're in a storm but you've been through many before and survived. You will survive this one too. As for the baby, we cannot say for sure if your smoking or drinking will have any impact on its health, right now. However, if it was only once, the chances are slim."

"Thank you, Dr. West."

She stands up and gives me a hug.

"I can do your initial work up today with bloodwork and prenatal vitamins and we can wait until you've made your decision before we do an ultrasound and listen for the heartbeat. How does that sound?"

I put my hand on my stomach, close my eyes and take a deep breath as tears fall.

I feel Dr. West's hand over mind.

"God, we trust your will. Strengthen Lynn now so she hears from you. Give her clarity of mind and peace. If anyone can understand and hear her heart, it's you. Have your way. Amen."

"Amen."

"I'll give you a few minutes."

"No Dr. West," I say grabbing her arm. "I've made my decision."

Leaving the doctor's office, I drive around for a while before stopping by the pharmacist for my prescription. I decide to park downtown at the river for a few minutes by myself. I turn off the engine and lock the doors before grabbing my phone to play some music through the Bluetooth.

Laying my head on the seat, the song Cycles by Jonathan McReynolds begins to play.

"Didn't I conquer this last year? Tell me what I missed cause I fear that it's coming back up again. Must be something I ate, some song, some show, some hate. The devil wants to extend the game, free throws and when it ends he wants to make the sequel cause if he has another chance. He feels like he can take my joy, my peace, my faith. See the devil, he learns from your mistakes even if you don't. That's how he keeps you in cycles, cycles, cycles, cycles but I'm not going in cycles, cycles."

I get home and grab a bottle of water from the refrigerator, some yogurt and a slice of chopped ham.

"Hey mom." Lilly says walking in the kitchen. "What's for dinner?"

"Um, how about some takeout? Order whatever and use my card."

"You okay?" She asks.

"Yea but I'm going to lay down for a minute." I tell her getting a plastic spoon and my prescription before walking into the bedroom. Sitting on the side of the bed, I read the instructions and swallow the pill before eating the ham then the yogurt.

I kick off my shoes and lay across the bed.

An hour or so later, I jump from my sleep and cry out in pain.

"Mom?" Lilly cries running into the room.

"I'm okay Lilly."

I cringe again, pulling my legs toward me.

"You're not okay." She says walking to the end of the bed. "What's wrong?"

"I'm fine."

"MOM, you're bleeding! I'm calling dad." She says running out the room.

I try to stop her but the pain will not let me say anything, so I get up and go into the bathroom and close the door to keep her from hearing me cry.

Jerome

"Is this seat taken?"

I look up, from my stool at the bar inside Marlowe's where I have been nursing my second or third Hennessy and Coke.

"No, it's all yours."

"I'm Victoria." She says extending her hand.

"Jerome."

"You seem sad Jerome. Did your dog die?"

"Something like that." I tell her.

"I am sorry to hear that." She motions for the bartender. "I'll have what he has and bring him another."

"Oh no," I wave at the bartender, "I'm good."

"You can't have a drink with me when I'm buying? Is that a way to treat a girl on her first night in the United States?"

I nod at the bartender agreeing to the drink. "Where are you from?"

"England." She smiles.

"And what brings you to Memphis?"

"Elvis." We both say together before laughing.

"Yea. I've been promising my mum I'd bring her for the last two years."

"Mum?" I repeat mimicking her accent. "Where is your mum now?"

She turns. "Over there doing Elvis karaoke."

She turns back and grabs her drink, taking a sip. "Wow is this what men drink in Memphis?"

"Only the real men." I reply.

"Well here's to a real man."

We spend the next few hours drinking and laughing at the people doing the bad Elvis impersonations, occasionally discussing our personal lives. I tell her a little about my troubles at home and she tells me about her boring, as she puts it, life of being a stay-at-home mom.

I look at my watch to see it's a little after ten.

"I better get going." I reach for my wallet and hand my card to the bartender before pressing the button on my phone to see its dead. I slide it in my pocket. "Thank you for taking my mind off my troubles."

"Thank you for keeping me company." Victoria replies.

I wait for the bartender to bring me the receipt. I sign it and stand up from the bar stool. Instead of walking out, I go and use the restroom first. When I am done, I head for the door but stop when I see Victoria waving for me to stop.

"Is everything okay?"

"Do you mind walking me to my room?" She asks. "As you can see, my mum and her friends aren't ready to go."

"Sure."

We walk outside, and she points to the hotel across the street. "That's where we're staying."

"How about we take my truck?"

"You're not a serial killer, are you?"

"Only on the weekends."

She laughs.

I pop the lock and we both get in. I make the two-minute drive to the hotel.

"Pull up to that gate."

I reach for her room key, but she leans over the console, allowing her dress to fall off her shoulder to reveal no bra. She reaches out the window and I take in the smell of her perfume.

Before she sits back, she licks across my lips and smiles. "You can pull up over there."

I put the truck in park and reach for the handle to get out and open her door.

"Wait." She says. "Do you mind helping me with something first?"

"Sure."

She pushes up and whispers in my ear.

"No, I can't do that." I say, throat getting dry. "I better go."

"Do you really need too? According to what you said earlier, you're already in trouble, a little more couldn't hurt."

"Yea, it could if my wife finds out." I say putting my hands on her shoulders to push her back.

"There is nobody here but us and I'll be back in England, in two days." Her hand is rubbing down the front of my pants. "You never have to see me again."

"No, I can't."

"Well, how about you just sit there and don't participate and I'll do all the heavy lifting."

She begins to unbuckle my pants. When I feel her hands roaming inside, I tense up.

"Shall I stop?"

I shake my head.

Thirty minutes later, I watch Victoria walk into the hotel before I berate myself for making another mistake.

"It's just oral, relax." I hear her voice saying in my head. *"You never have to see me again."*

"What is wrong with you?" I ask to the open air. "God, what is wrong with me?"

Lynn

I open my eyes to see my mom sitting on the bed and Lilly asleep on the couch.

"Mom, what are you doing here?"

"Lilly called me because she was worried about you. She said you were bleeding and in a lot of pain but by the time I got here, you were asleep."

"I told her I was okay. She shouldn't have called you."

"She was scared Lynn and she tried calling Jerome but he didn't answer. What's going on?" She asks. "And don't lie to me."

Her raising her voice causes Lilly to sit up.

"Mom, you okay? I'm sorry for calling grandma but I was worried. You were in a lot of pain."

I run into the bathroom. The cramping isn't as bad as it was before but my stomach feels like I have a virus.

"Lynn are you okay?"

"Yes mom, give me a minute and I'll explain." I tell her.

I stay another ten minutes before washing my hand and opening the door. Lilly is sitting at the foot of the bed and mom standing next to her.

"Where is Mallory and Nathaniel?"

"She's asleep and he's playing his game." My mom answers. "Now explain."

"I had a miscarriage." I tell them. "The pain and the bleeding and now upset stomach is a part of what I have to go through, but I am fine."

"You were pregnant? Why didn't you say something?" Mom asks.

"I found out in the midst of everything going on and when I went to the doctor today, she couldn't find a heartbeat."

Lilly has tears in her eyes.

"I'm okay Lilly." I say wiping her face.

"I'm sorry about the baby." She hugs me, tight.

"Please don't mention this to your brother and sister because I don't want them to worry about me.

Now, go to bed because you have to get up early in the morning. Thank you for taking care of me and I love you."

"I love you too mom. Goodnight Grams."

When she leaves, I look over to my mom.

"Are you really okay?"

I shake my head no. "I am trying but I feel like I am about to lose my mind. I'm so angry mom."

"Angry at who?"

"Jerome, God, me. Hell, take your pick." I tell her. "Why is this happening to me?"

She doesn't say anything.

"Mom?"

"I hear you but I'm waiting until you are done with your tantrum before I say anything. Go on and get it out."

"You don't understand." I say getting back into the bed.

"How do you know what I do or don't understand? Have you asked? Little girl, you aren't the first person to be cheated on and neither are you the first to face trouble. This is called life and, in this life, shit happens. What are you going to do about it?"

"It hurts." I cry.

"It's supposed to hurt, how else would you know you're going through anything if it didn't? That doesn't mean you give up. Child, if I gave up every time something hurt, I wouldn't be where I am or half the woman I am today. James said in--"

"No bible, please."

"Hush and listen. James says in James one, count it all joy, my brothers, when you meet trials of various kinds, for you know that the testing of your faith produces steadfastness. And let steadfastness have its full effect, that you may be perfect and complete, lacking in nothing."

"Yea, well I am having a hard time finding joy in all of this."

"Joy is not lost Lynn, but it is buried by the junk you have covered it with." She gets up and walks over to me, pulling me into her arms. "Baby, I know you are hurting and it doesn't seem like it will end but it will after it has run its course. You cannot rush it because if you do, then you run the risk of miscarrying."

I cry into her chest.

"I know it hurts, physically and spiritually but you have to trust God's plan. In the meantime, you worship and trust God, even when it does not make sense. Why? Because it confuses the enemy. Baby, you are not promised to reap a bountiful harvest, every season but that does not mean you don't plant one because the seeds that didn't grow this time, still have potential to grow next time."

I push away from her. "Mom, why are you talking in parables like Jesus? I don't want to be preached too, not tonight, can't I just have my mom? I am at the edge and I need you!"

"And I am right here, trying to get you to see that Jesus is exactly who you need at a time like this. Lynn, you're at the edge but you haven't fallen. You want to know why?"

I sigh before sitting on the side of the bed. "No mom, why haven't I fallen?"

"Because God loves us, and He shields us when we are too selfish to see we need it. He protects us, even when we are playing patty cake with our prayers and the enemy persuades us into thinking we got wings and can fly. You thought you could do this on your own, yet your silly self came to the edge and now you're fearful. But God is right here at the edge with you while you waddle through what you're dealing with. Yes, your marriage is on the brink and you lost a baby but you are still alive with three beautiful children who love you, a roof over your head, money in the bank and in your right mind. That should be enough for you to walk away from the edge." She tells me.

"What about this anger?"

"Deal with it but do so from the root or you will never get over it. And while you deal with, do not sin. You can cry but don't sin. You can yell but don't sin. You can even break some stuff but don't sin."

"Man, you are always in preach mode but thank you. I needed to hear every word you said."

"Yes, you did." She says walking over to give me a hug. "Now, get some rest and I'll be by tomorrow to check on you."

She turns out the light in my room and I hear her set the alarm. I slide down under the covers where I allow the tears to fall.

"God, please forgive me for thinking I could do this without you and thank you for never leaving me. Thank you for keeping me from falling when I know I have done and said some things I shouldn't have. Thank you, God, for protecting me even while I'm standing at the edge acting like I don't need you. Truth is God, I need you more than ever because I can't do it on my own. Please God, I know I've done wrong but don't take your joy from me. Instead, guide me to the place you will have me to be. God, I apologize for trying to do what only you can and I surrender to you, now, every part of me. Have your way. Amen."

Jerome

I walk into the house to see Lynn cooking breakfast.

"It smells good in here." I tell her.

"What are you doing here?"

"I had to meet with Lee, at the construction site of the new school, to go over some permits and since I was in the area, I decided to come here and get some clothes."

"Well, I am sure the kids will be happy to see you. If you want to stay and have breakfast with them, it will be ready in a few minutes." She says pulling biscuits from the oven.

"Can I take a shower?"

"Sure. In the guest room."

I walk into our bedroom to get some clothes from the closet. I stop when I get inside the door and look at the new bed and it makes me remember when we first moved in.

"Boy, you're going to break this cheap bed, get down." Lynn laughs when I jump on the bed.

"So, I'll just buy another one with the check we are getting next week and then we can break it too."

"Oh, you must think you got bed breaking capabilities Mr. Watson?"

"Why don't I show you, Mrs. Watson."

"Come on then big daddy."

I take a step and the bed crashes to the floor. I catch myself from falling before looking back at Lynn who burst out laughing.

"I guess I'm going shopping."

"Hey, are you okay?" Lynn asks pulling me out of my thoughts.

I quickly wipe my face.

"Do you remember the very first bed we had, when we moved in this house?"

"The one you didn't want to get rid of although it was being held up by wood sticks you made from two by fours? I remember."

"I couldn't get rid of it because it was the first thing we bought in both of our names."

"Until you broke it by jumping on it."

I laugh. "Man, we had some great times, didn't we?" I say as my eyes fill, again, with tears. "I'm sorry for messing everything up."

"Well, no sense in dwelling on what has happened when we can't change it." She says walking out.

I stand there a few seconds longer before grabbing some underwear, a t-shirt and sweat pants.

After my shower, I go into the kitchen. I speak to Lilly but she doesn't answer.

"Lilly are you okay?"

"Mom, can I eat in my room?" She asks Lynn, never looking in my direction.

"Not until you stop being disrespectful to your dad. You know better."

"Fine, I'm not hungry then." She yells, dropping the plate on the table.

"Hold on, what is wrong with you?" I ask.

"YOU! You're what's wrong with me. It's bad enough that you cheat on mom but not being here when she needs you is low, very low, even for you." She screams.

"What are you talking about? Please calm down and tell me."

She wipes her face with the sleeve of her pajama top. "It doesn't matter now."

She stomps out.

Before I can ask Lynn about Lilly's actions, Mallory and Nathaniel come rushing in.

"Daddy," Mallory squeals.

"Hey pumpkin, how are you?"

"Good." She says giving me a hug while Nathaniel walks over and starts fixing his plate.

"Nathaniel, you can't speak to your old man?"

"What's up?" He answers.

"You think you and I can talk later?"

"Sure." He shrugs.

I turn to see Lynn handing me a plate.

"Thank you. Are you not eating?"

"Maybe later. I'm going to lay down."

I watch her walk out.

Mallory, Nathaniel and I eat together. By the time we are done, Lilly comes in and begins to clean the kitchen while Nathaniel and I go out on the back porch to talk.

"I saw you." He blurts.

"What do you mean?"

"I saw you, one day, with that woman. It was the day you came to my soccer practice. You thought I'd gone in the building but I forgot one of my knee pads. When I came out, I saw her getting into your car and you pulled off."

"Why didn't you say anything?"

"I didn't want to hurt mom." He says. "But it was hard carrying around this secret. It hurt but I couldn't bear to give mom another reason to cry."

I try to put my arm around him, but he moves.

"Nathaniel, I messed up. I never meant to hurt y'all but I made a mistake. Can you please forgive me?"

"Has mom forgiven you?" He asks.

"That's a question you will have to ask her, but your forgiveness is yours to give. Look, I am not proud of the shame I bought to my family. I let you down, being my only son and I'm sorry. I never want you to think that my actions are the way you should treat a woman because they are not."

"Dad, you are human and will make mistakes, but I expected you to be a man about them."

I look at him with my eyebrows raised.

"I am almost sixteen years old, so I get that mistakes happen. You all have been telling us this our entire life but how can you expect us to own up to our mistakes, as children, if you don't as adults? You are supposed to set an example for us."

"Wow." I say.

"Look dad, you disappointed me but I still love you and I forgive you. I don't know if you and mom are considering divorce but if you are, don't allow it to change the relationship you have with us. All we can do now is move forward and try to heal."

My mouth is open, but no words will come out. He stands up from the patio steps and holds out his arms to me. I stand up and give him a hug.

When he releases me, I step back.

"I am so proud of you." I tell him.

"Thank you." He smiles. "You and mom raised me right, just don't let me down again."

"Yes sir." I say, still shocked by the entire conversation.

He raises his fist and I connect mine with his before he walks back into the house.

I sit back on the steps, replaying the conversation with Nathaniel or should I say, the conversation Nathaniel had with me.

I close my eyes as the tears sting my face.

"God, please forgive me for all the pain I have caused. Thank you for covering and protecting my family. Although I don't know what tomorrow holds for us, I trust you with all of me. Amen."

I walk into the house and to the bedroom door. I raise my hand to knock but decide against it.

Lynn

I walk into the church with the children. They all disburse to their meeting groups and I head towards the sanctuary for the women's group bible study. I peek inside and hear them doing devotion so I go to use the restroom.

It's been a week since the miscarriage and my body is starting to feel normal again. I still need to talk to Jerome about it and I will but tonight, I am here to be fed spiritually because I've been missing worship.

Coming out of the restroom, I see Sharon Matthews, the wife of Deacon Raymond Matthews and Erica waiting to go into the sanctuary. When she sees me, she tells Erica to go inside.

"Lynn, hey, can I speak to you for a moment?" She asks.

"Sure Sharon, what's up?"

She motions for me to follow her to the usher room, near the sanctuary.

"As you know Erica is pregnant with Raymond's baby."

"Unhuh." I nod.

"Well, we've asked her to move in with us."

"Okay but why are you telling me?" I ask with a bewildered look on my face.

"Nobody knows about the affair she had with my husband, other than you, Jerome, Pastor and his wife so we've been telling people she's a surrogate seeing I can't have children of my own."

"That's great Sharon, congratulations."

"I wanted you to know in case anyone asks, you know so we'll have the same story." She says. "Plus, I don't want you to feel uncomfortable being around her."

"Sharon look, whatever you do with your life is your business. If you and Erica want to become sister-wives, have at it. As far as speaking about any of this mess, I don't plan on it. And don't worry about me feeling uncomfortable because you and I are not friends to even hang out. The only advice I'll give is, be careful."

I walk pass her into the sanctuary, a little ticked off that she has made me miss the first few minutes of bible study.

I find a seat and ask the young lady what book of the bible we're in.

"Exodus 14:14." She says.

"Thanks."

I turn to the passage and chills go over me.

The LORD shall fight for you, and ye shall hold your peace.

"Ladies, tonight this scripture is for a few of you who feels like you're on the edge." Pastor Karen says. "Many of you have showed up tonight because you felt like you had nothing to lose and surely nothing to gain. Why? Because you're at the edge. Yep! You are backed up at the edge of give up and one more push of the gas pedal will send you over. Let me ask you a question, what's stopping you?"

I look around to see a few ladies dabbing their eyes.

Pastor Karen continues. "What's keeping you from giving up? Is it the children, the husband, the dog or the cat?"

A few women chuckle.

"Let's be honest with ourselves, shall we? Some of you have yet to give up because you're scared of what it looks like it. If you give up your marriage what will being single look like? If you quit your job, what will it look like? I can tell you this, it can either look worse than your current circumstance or better but what do you have to lose other than your mind, if you stay where you are? I get it, pain and anger pushed you to the edge and you want to lash out but Exodus 14:14 shares, the LORD shall fight for you, and ye shall hold your peace."

"But what does that mean?" A lady asks.

"Good question." Pastor Karen says. "Peace, biblically, means to be complete or to live well. So, this scripture says, if you allow God to fight for you, you'll remain complete not broken and capable of living well and not distressed. See, when we try to fight stuff on our own, we mess up but when we stand still and allow God to fight for us, we hold our peace for it is peace that allows us to live well."

"What happens if the fight doesn't end the way we think it should?" I question.

"If you've allowed God to fight for you then it'll end the way that fits with what God has for your life and He doesn't make mistakes. We do but God doesn't."

Bible study continues and by the time it is over, I am feeling refreshed. I grab my things to wait on the kids.

"Lynn," Pastor Karen calls out. "Hey, I just wanted to give you a hug and tell you how happy I am to see you."

"Thank you. Your message was great tonight and I am glad I came."

"Me too. How is everything?"

"It's too hard for me so I'm holding my peace and letting God fight it." I tell her.

"He's the best one to relinquish it too." She says before someone calls her name. "Well, I am here if there is anything I can do even if it's just to listen."

"Thank you, Pastor Karen."

The kids finally come and we head home, stopping by Abbay's Soul Food to pick up some dinner.

"How was bible study?" Jerome asks when we walk into the house.

"Great, good, it was okay." He laughs at the different responses from the children.

"I talked to Pastor Carrington tonight and they have decided to engrave a pew in honor of Pastor Sydney." He says to me.

The kids all grab their food.

"Do not leave those food containers in your rooms." Jerome says to their backs of the children as they disburse. "How was bible study for you?"

"Why are you here?"

"Lynn, I want to come home. It is hard staying in hotels day after day. Please, I'll sleep in the guest room."

"For how long?"

"Until I can find an apartment or house to rent."

"Six months." I tell him.

"Thank you."

I grab my food and get ready to walk out.

"Babe wait, can we talk about what you're going to do about the baby? You haven't said anything since your appointment and that's been over a week."

"I lost the baby."

He follows me into the bedroom.

"Why didn't you tell me?" He says.

"Because I've been trying to come to terms with it." I say sitting the food on the nightstand. "And you haven't been here."

"You could have called!" He says raising his voice causing me to look at him. "I'm sorry for yelling. What happened?"

I sigh. "Dr. West did some bloodwork and my hormone levels were extremely low, so she performed an ultrasound and there was no heartbeat."

"Okay so what happens now?"

"Nothing. She gave me a pill and I miscarried."

"Lynn, you should have told me."

I stop and turn around towards him. "I should have told you?" I laugh. "It's funny you say that because Lilly tried to call you, the night it happened. She called you over and over because she saw me bleeding and was scared. However, just like this new Jerome, we all know, you weren't there but you popped in that Saturday, three days later, for clothes like a roommate."

"Is that why Lilly has been upset with me?"

"No Jerome, she genuinely doesn't like you." I say being sarcastic. "What do you think? You promised this mess between us wouldn't change your relationship with them and it has. Already."

"I didn't know."

"Yea, that's been your favorite excuse, as of late but what's done is done. I am dealing with the pain of miscarrying our baby the same as I am dealing with the pain of you failing our marriage; alone."

"I'm sorry."

"I am not the one you need to be apologizing too. Go and talk to your daughter."

He pauses but then turns to walk out.

Jerome

Sunday morning, I get up early, make a cup of coffee and go out to sit on the back porch.

"I dealt with the pain of miscarrying our baby the same as I am dealing with the pain of you failing our marriage; alone."

I replay Lynn's words in my head. I turn when I hear the door open.

"Hey, why are you up so early?" I ask Lynn.

"Couldn't sleep." She says pulling her robe closed before sitting on the couch next to me. "What about you?"

"Same. I've been thinking about what you said the other night and I am so sorry I wasn't there for you when you miscarried the baby. I apologized to Lilly too."

"Good but please stop apologizing to me because I'm sick of hearing it and it doesn't help or fix anything. What's done is done."

I exhale before sitting back. "I don't know what else to do."

"Look, I didn't come out here to argue with you, I came for some air and to talk to God. Truth is, I can careless what you do, when it comes to your personal life but don't allow it to interfere with your relationship with your children. They are the only reason I am allowing you to stay here."

"Lynn, I know I've hurt you but do you really hate me this much?"

"I don't hate you but I surely dislike this person you have become." She says.

"I made a mistake because I am human. It doesn't take away everything we've been through and neither does it change my heart. I am still the same person."

"Are you?"

"Of course I am." I look at her. "Babe, where do we go from here? How are we supposed to do life apart when we've been together most of our life?"

"We figure it out, one minute at a time."

"Do you think we can remain friends for the sake of the children?" I ask.

"As much as I want to say no, we have too but you hurt me Jerome. You hurt me deeply and although I love you with every fiber of my being; the hurt, shame and pain caused by your infidelity has scarred me." She says getting up. "And right now, I don't know what to do with it. All I do know is, we cannot remain married."

I look out over the back yard without responding.

"There is something else I need to tell you."

She sits back down.

"Nathaniel knew about the affair. He saw me and Mattie together at his soccer practice."

She doesn't say anything as tears fall from her eyes.

"Lynn, please say something."

"What am I supposed to say to that Jerome? Huh? What could I possibly say in response to that?"

She gets up and I watch her walk into the house.

"Damn it!" I scream picking up my coffee cup and throwing it across the back yard.

I sit out there a while longer, getting my emotions in check before going to find Lynn. I walk into the bedroom to see her sitting on the couch writing in her journal.

I close the door.

"Jerome--"

"I am so sorry Lynn."

"Jerome, please stop apologizing!" She says closing the journal and throwing it on the couch. "You're sorry, I get that, but it cannot fix what has been broken and I am not about to spend another second pretending it will. You put our family in a hard place. I can't even imagine the guilt Nathaniel has been carrying with that secret. My only son knew his dad was cheating but couldn't say anything because he feels the weight of protecting me. Can you imagine how that makes me feel?"

I sit on the floor across from her with my back against the bed and my head in my hand as I listen to her cry.

"He shouldn't have to protect me from crap like that Jerome. He's only fifteen."

"I know."

"Do you? Do you truly know what your selfishness has done to us?"

I cry into my arm.

"I am so sorry Lynn."

She stands over me, putting her hand on my head.

"I know." She says sniffling. "But now I need to get ready for church and you need to get out."

Breaking News

A 37 -year-old female has died, after committing suicide in her cell at the Shelby County Jail East Women's Facility. Madeline Perez had been incarcerated at the facility on charges of murder. If you remember, Perez was indicted for the brutal hit-and-run of Sydney Gable, a youth pastor, who was killed July 19, 2018. She was being held on no bond until her trial which was scheduled to begin in November.

Authorities say, Perez was alive, at the facility at 2700 Sycamore Ave., during the last count at midnight but jail staff found her unresponsive about 6:30 a.m. According to the statement released, Memphis Fire Department personnel was called in and attempted life saving measures but were unsuccessful.

News Channel 22's Raven Turner, spoke with Sherriff Eric Sussex who stated, Perez was not on suicide watch and that an investigation into her death will be conducted. More information will be released when it becomes available.

Lynn

Walking out of the gym, I see Mateo standing next to my car.

I roll my eyes.

"What do you want?"

"I don't know if you heard about Mattie but she's dead."

"Man cut the crap because everybody with a TV knows Mattie is dead so what do you really want?"

"I wanted to apologize to you again."

"Apology accepted. Goodbye."

"I am leaving tomorrow to take Mattie's body to Mexico for burial and I didn't want to leave without apologizing for everything that has happened. I am so sorry. Maybe if I'd gotten Mattie some help, none of us would have gone through any of this."

"Well, it's kind of too late for would haves, don't you think? Anyway, for the sake of the other passengers on the plane, have a safe flight."

I open my car door.

"Lynn, I was wondering if you and I can get coffee when I get back in a few weeks."

"Are you serious? Do you honestly think I'd sit anywhere with you to have anything?"

"I know you're still upset but-"

"One sec." I say pulling out my phone.

I hold the home button down for a second. "Siri, how do you say screw you and go to hell in Spanish?"

"Atornillarte e irte al infierno," Siri recites.

"One more time," I say pressing the button to hear it again. "Atornillarte e irte al infierno. And to make sure we're clear, let me say it in English. Screw you and go to hell!"

I get in, start the car and drive off.

Turning onto my street, I see a car parked in front of my house. I slowly drive by and see its Erica.

"Really God?" I question parking in the garage. "What can I do for you?" I ask when she walks up the driveway.

"I have a letter, for you, from Mattie." She says handing me an envelope.

"I don't want anything from her. Now, get out of my driveway."

"She wasn't always like this." Erica states stopping me from walking off.

"Let me guess, she's had a hard life. Well newsflash Erica, we've all had it hard, but it doesn't mean you sleep with other people's husbands, pretend to be their friend for fun and make a mockery of another person's pain. Oh, my bad, I forgot who I'm talking too when you've been doing the same thing."

"You're right. I was sleeping with a married man but that does not make me a bad person."

I chuckle. "You may not be a bad person however you have bad intentions when it comes to people. But let me ask you, why are you bringing me this letter now and she's dead?"

"It came in the mail yesterday. I didn't know she was planning to take her life because she hadn't spoken to me since everything happened, but I hope she finds peace in death that she couldn't get on earth."

"Oh, that's nice of you to say. Is there anything else?"

"I only came to bring you this letter because it was her last request."

"Aww, I should feel obligated to read it now. Um, no thanks, we've established what you can do with that letter."

She fidgets with her purse strap. "I'm sorry Lynn. I knew Mattie was sleeping with Jerome but I didn't know he was married until that Sunday I came to the church. After service was over, I confronted him and her because I didn't agree with what they were doing, in your face."

"Why didn't you tell me?" I ask.

"It wasn't my place. Look, I've known Mattie since I was thirteen. She and Mateo were in the same foster home I ended up in and we connected. They have been my only family."

"Family? Family sleep with each other because at the club, you acted like you were dating."

"Her kissing me is nothing new. We've shared beds and men before."

"So, was this like some kind of con or something?"

"No, it was supposed to be fun with no feelings involved. I was to sleep with Raymond to get him off Jerome because he was becoming suspicious of him and Mattie but then we started having feelings for one another and I ended up pregnant."

"Isn't that nice." I say sarcastically.

"I never thought Mattie would go as far as she did. I knew she loved Jerome but I kept telling her, he'd never leave you. Anyway, I'm sorry. I only came to give you this letter because she requested. It's sealed so I don't know what it says. Will you please take it and read it?"

"No thank you. Whatever she had to say, she should have said it before she attempted to kill me.

And before you come here again, stop and think, what would Jesus do and stay the hell away from me."

Looking at my watch to see I have about an hour before our family session with Dr. Mitchell. I rush into the house to the TV's volume high and Mattie and Lilly dancing to some game. I drop my keys and water bottle on the table and head down the hall.

It takes about thirty minutes but I am changed and ready.

"Let's go." I scream to the kids.

Jerome

"Good afternoon Jerome, you're here early. We have about thirty minutes before Lynn and the children get here so you can wait out here or in my office."

"I came early because I wanted to talk to you first, alone." I tell her.

"Okay, then come in. Can I get you something to drink?"

"No thanks."

"I know this isn't, technically our session but I'd still like to begin with prayer."

We grab hands.

"God, once again you have allowed us to gather in this room of restoration. I ask you to destroy anything that is not like you as we seek to be made whole. Gather our wayward thoughts so they do not impede on the healing needed and use me God, for I am only the vessel. Speak through me with your power so it is clear you are the one in charge. Bless this young man who has returned that he may find peace during his storm. Amen."

We sit.

"Tell me--"

"Lynn and I are going through with the divorce." I announce. "I am currently sleeping in the guest room of the house until I can find a new place. Lilly is half speaking to me, Nathaniel knew I was having an affair and Lynn lost the baby."

"Wow. Okay," She responds taking a breath. "Those are a lot of changes in a short amount of time. How are you coping?"

"Honestly, Dr. Mitchell I don't know. It seems like I am walking around in a fog that will not clear. I know I did this to my family, but I don't know how to come out of this dark place I'm in because apologizing isn't helping."

"You come out by putting one foot in front of the other and moving." She tells me. "I get that you feel the need to apologize, over and over but you've done that. Leave it up to Lynn and the children to forgive you but in the meantime, you must forgive yourself. Otherwise, you'll stay in the dark place you've sentenced yourself too."

"How can I forgive myself when I see the turmoil my actions have caused?"

"I assumed you all have talked to the children about your decision to divorce and this is the reason Lilly is upset. She's the oldest, right?"

"Yes but no, she's upset because I wasn't there when Lynn miscarried the baby."

"She felt like you let her down again."

"But I would have been there had I known. My phone died and--"

"Jerome," Dr. Mitchell interrupts. "You don't have to explain."

"I don't know what else to do."

"What about the other children?"

"Nathaniel told me he knew about the affair, but he forgives me." I say as tears fall. "He, um, he forgave me for making one of the biggest mistakes of my life and Mallory seems to be okay."

"What about Lynn? How is she handling everything?"

"She doesn't talk to me about it, anymore. She did allow me to move back home, in the guest room and we talk about business and the children but that's it."

"So, everybody survived?"

"What do you mean?"

"Everybody in your family seems to be handling the mistakes you dealt them except you. They are moving on but you're still stuck. Why?"

I get up and walk over to the window. "I don't know how! I'm angry for what I did but I'm also mad at Lynn for giving up on me so easily."

"You think she gave up easily?"

"I thought some time apart and maybe a few more sessions with you would get her to forgive me but she hasn't. I asked her to give us time to work this out and she won't. I made one mistake out of eighteen years of marriage and it's over like a puff of smoke. Am I not entitled to one mistake?"

"So, you're the victim?" She states more like a sentence than a question.

"No but I have feelings too." I say walking back to the couch and sitting down.

"Jerome, you cannot be the victim in the crime you committed. You must be held accountable for your part in what happened, take the sentence and do the time. Unfortunately for you, your crime destroyed your marriage but you can salvage the relationship."

"I can't see her with another man."

"There it is." She smirks. "Finally, the truth. It's not that you made a mistake, hurt your wife and children, destroyed your home but you can't stomach Lynn being to another man what she has been to you?"

"I can still make her happy!" I yell. "I did for twenty plus years of us being together."

"Jerome, reality is, you used to make her happy and it is quite possible you could again but is that what Lynn wants? Look, I don't know what the future holds for you and Lynn. She could forgive you and call off the divorce or she forgives you and still divorces you. Either way, you need to man up my brother and be ready for which ever one she chooses."

"Don't I get a choice?"

"Yes, a choice of how you'll survive after her choice."

"I thought you were supposed to help me."

"Help is only received when you willingly accept it and until you come out of the sunken place you're in, you will not receive the help I can offer you. Right now, you want me to pacify you but I can't do that and if you keep seeing things, from a selfish point of view, you are dangerous."

"Dangerous, to who?" I inquire, confused by her words.

"Yourself more than Lynn. See, you are suffering from an undiagnosed condition called, CHIA, C-H-I-A or can't have it all. Men like you, who suffer from this condition, have trouble surviving when they can't have it all, so you become dangerous.

It doesn't mean you'll physically hurt yourself or somebody, but your heart and demeanor will turn cold and you'll set out to hurt folk before they hurt you."

I look off. "I don't want to be that person Dr. Mitchell."

"Then you need to overcome this thinking like the victim. Sure, your dad may have been abusive, but you've shown the strength to overcome that. You may have had an affair that destroyed your marriage, but you can overcome that too--"

"Dr. Mitchell, the Watson family is here." My secretary interrupts.

"We can finish this in another session, if you choose."

She walks over to her desk.

"Please send them back."

Family Restoration Session | Dr. Mitchell

"Good afternoon, you must be Lilly, Mallory and Nathaniel?"

They all nod and smile. Lynn walks in and stops when she sees Jerome.

"I was just calling you." She tells him.

"I came early." He replies.

"Would anybody like something to drink?' I question.

Everyone says no.

"Okay, then let us pray. Dear God, we thank you for another chance to petition your throne. Thank you for the family who has gathered here and now I must ask for your guidance. Come in and have your way. Bless us as we seek peace, understanding and most of all forgiveness to while we travel this road of restoration. Amen."

"Amen."

We all sit, and I pick up my iPad. I look at each one of them and notice the nervousness and tension.

"Before we begin, I want everybody to take a breath. In and out." I wait until they are done. "Now, I know it may feel weird to be in a room, with your mom and dad, discussing your feelings but it is only to help each of you." I say to the children. "I don't want you to feel overwhelmed. Okay?"

They look at each other.

"Let me start by asking whose idea was it to come here today, as a family?"

"Mine," Lynn says.

"And what do you hope to achieve with this session today Lynn?" I ask her.

"Closure." She states. "Not as in finality but closing the door on all that has happened lately because it didn't just affect Jerome and I, it did them as well. They are hurting although they've done a great job at covering it and as long as we keep harping on the mistakes, we will never move on."

I look at them.

"Do you all agree with what your mom said?"

They nod.

"Lilly, I hear you're upset with your dad. Tell me why."

She has her arms folded across her chest. "He wasn't there for my mom. I called him over and over and he never showed up."

"I explained to Lilly that I didn't get your call. My phone was dead."

"No Jerome don't make excuses just apologize." I tell him.

"Lilly, I apologize for not being there. Will you forgive me?"

"You said the divorce wasn't going to keep you from being there for us and you aren't even divorced yet and it already has." She cries. "You lied!"

I motion for Jerome to go to her. He kneels, taking her hand. "You are right, and I am sorry. I did not keep my promise, but I shouldn't have made that promise to begin with. Can we start over?"

She shrugs.

"From now on, this is to each of you," Jerome says looking at the children, "I can't say I will not mess up again but I don't plan on it. Yes, your mom and I are getting a divorce but I will be there as much as I can. I love each of you and I pray you will forgive me and allow me time to make up what I've messed up. Will you do that?"

"Lilly, Nathaniel and Mallory, do you accept your dad's apology?"

They each hunch their shoulders.

"We will take that as a tentative yes."

Jerome pulls her up into a hug and she reluctantly hugs him back.

"I forgive you daddy." Mallory says. "I just don't like it when you make mom cry and she used to cry a lot, so we'd take turns sitting outside her room, in case she needed us."

"Lynn, did you know that?" I inquire.

Lynn wipes her eyes before laying her hand on Mallory's arm. "I did. I used to hear them."

"Whose idea was it to sit outside her door?" I question.

They point at Nathaniel.

"Nathaniel, why sit outside your mom's door instead of going in?"

"I knew she'd never let us see her cry, so I wanted us to be there because she didn't have anybody. We have each other," he says looking at his sisters, "but mom was alone."

"I am never alone as long as I have you guys." Lynn says. "And while I appreciate you all wanting to be there for me, I don't ever want you to feel obligated to take care of me. I am the mom-"

"And it's your job to worry about us." Lilly interjects. "But not everything can be done on your own mom. You need to let us help."

"You are right."

"I want us to do an exercise." I say getting up. "I am going to give each of you an index card and pen. On the front of the card I want you to write one thing you would change about somebody in the room and on the back, I want you to write one thing you are willing to change about yourself."

I give them ten minutes to finish the exercise.

"Is everybody done? Who wants to go first and tell us who you chose, the one thing you'd change about them and then the thing you'd change about yourself."

Nathaniel raises his hand.

"Nathaniel, the floor is yours."

"I chose my mom and the one thing I would change about her is the way she keeps everything bottled up. The bible says in Romans 15:1, "We who are strong have an obligation to bear with the failings of the weak and not to please ourselves."" He pauses. "Mom, I'm almost sixteen and I know I can't take dad's place but I'm strong enough for you to lean on."

I pass Lynn the box of Kleenex as he continues.

"As for me, I will change the amount of time I spend playing my video games to be there for my mom and sisters when dad is not there. That's it."

I swallow my emotions. "Who's next?"

"I'll go." Mallory says. "I chose Nathaniel, but he already beat me to what I wanted to say. As for me, I will clean my room more so mom doesn't have to holler about it."

We all laugh as Lilly stands.

"I pick my dad. One thing I would change about him is the amount of time he works. Dad, we are older but it doesn't mean we need you any less. As for me, I'm going to change my choice of college. I was going to Spelman but now I want to stay here and help mom--"

"No Lilly." Lynn interrupts. "I guess you can figure out that my person is Lilly. If I could change one thing about her, it's her need to take care of everybody, especially me. You are going to Spelman, little girl and we will make sure of it by having you packed up and ready to go, in two weeks. The thing I would change about me is the need to hold everything in. I am an only child so doing everything on my own, is all I know but I will work on changing that."

"Jerome."

He clears his throat and stands as Lynn sits down.

"I didn't choose anybody because the person I would change is me. I don't have to go into my long list of flaws, but I am standing here before each of you saying, I will change the long hours I work and no matter what happens between us, I will be there for you." I pause. "These last five months, I wish I could do over but since I can't, I only ask for your forgiveness."

"How about we stop here for today." I say standing up. "Before I pray, I want you all to do something. I want each of you to look around. Do you see the people looking back at you? They're your family. These people will be there for you when nobody else will. These are the people you will count on and they may let you down, break a promise, upset you or even make you cry but they will be there. Don't ever take a person, in this room, for granted because none of us are promised tomorrow."

"Thank you, Dr. Mitchell."

"Lynn, read this for me, to your family."

I hand her the card and she stands.

"Be quiet, this time. Stop trying to fix, with your mouth, what your emotions destroyed. Instead pray and fast for God's direction then He'll give you the ability to walk in the newness only His mercy can provide. Be quiet, this time and fellowship with God so that He can restore your heart because whether you know it or not, your actions, from this day forward, dictates how the next person will treat you. Anger responds with anger, but a soft answer turns away wrath. Proverbs 14:1, The Message Bible says, Lady Wisdom builds a lovely home, sir fool comes along and tears it down break by break."

"Let us pray." I say. "God, thank you. Thank you for the ability to accept the things we've done wrong and for giving us another chance to repair them. I thank you God for Jerome, Lynn, Lilly, Nathaniel and Mallory for coming to seek help instead of trying to fix things on their own. I thank you for the time we've spent with you, in grace and I ask you to cover and protect this family like only you can because we know you have plans for them that was decided before they were formed in their mother's womb. God, do for this family what they need. I humbly submit this prayer in faith. Amen."

"Thank you, Dr. Mitchell."

"You're welcome and I look forward to seeing you all again."

Saying Goodbye

"We stand here today, amid pain, grief and broken hearts to say goodbye to our marriage. There are no right words to erase all that has happened and no magical clock to turn back time however we take joy in all the memories we have shared over the past twenty-five years." Jerome says.

"This is why we thank you God, even now because we know everything ordained by you is for a time and purpose. Thank you, God, for the lives created during this marriage. Thank you for the struggles and the sacrifices. Thank you for the good days that made our load lighter and for the bad that kept us up at night because they made us stronger." I say, wiping the tears. "We thank You Father that although our lives have changed, we have the abiding presence of Your Spirit that will strengthen and sustain us to make it through."

"And God, forgive me." Jerome cuts in. "Forgive me for breaking the covenant of our marriage. Forgive me for falling into temptation. Forgive me for making my wife feel unloved and for defiling our marriage bed. I can only pray that you clean and restore me to be the man you have destined me to be. Most of all, restore the heart of my wife that she may be able to love again without walls. Don't allow what I've done to destroy her chance at happiness. Amen."

I wipe my eyes. "May the God of peace, who through the blood of the eternal covenant paid for by the blood of our Lord Jesus, equip us with everything good for doing His will and may He work in us what is pleasing to Him?"

I burst into tears and Jerome comes over and grabs me in his arms.

"You were everything I needed. You were the butter to my biscuits, the gravy to my smothered chicken, the cream for my coffee, the cinnamon in the middle of my cinnamon roll and the light on the darkest days."

I laugh through my tears. Jerome squeezes me harder. "Forgive me Lynn, for everything."

"I do." I whisper.

"Will you promise not to change who you are?"

"I won't if you promise to not break another woman's heart." I tell him.

"I won't." Jerome answers. "As long as you promise to be my friend."

"I will."

He releases me and we walk over to the box I put together earlier. It has some of our wedding pictures and a few tokens we've collected over the years that we deemed necessary to end this season of our life. We put in the papers holding the "vows" we just finished reading and I stop before closing it.

"Jerome, we've had an amazing lifetime together. We have three beautiful children, a successful business and a house we paid off, in ten years. We've had some amazing celebrations and vacations. We've grown up together and our struggle taught us how to survive the toughest storms. We have experienced highs and lows and wins and losses. We've managed to save some money while creating a legacy our children and their children can continue. Jerome, we made it this far and even though our season is over, I thank you for all the seasons we experienced."

He kisses me on the lips and I allow him too.

I pull a piece of wood out. "Do you know what this is?"

He shakes his head.

"It's a piece of our old bed. I didn't know why God had me save it before but it makes sense now."

"How so?" He questions.

"Our marriage bed was defiled and when I wanted to be discouraged, God wouldn't allow it to taint my heart. I am putting this piece of wood in the box as a sign of being broken but not bitter, damaged but not destroyed and hurt but not helpless."

"Are y'all done yet?" Mallory hollers from the back door. "I'm hungry."

"Yes little girl, we are on our way in."

"What do you want to do with the box now that it's done?" Jerome asks.

"This is a funeral, so I am going to bury it."

"I'll get the shovel." He says.

"No, I'll do it later."

"Are you sure?"

"Yes, I need to."

*****

My alarm goes off at 11:30. I slide on some flip flops, turn off the alarm and go out into the back yard. I grab the shovel and the box, from the patio and walk over to the spot I picked out earlier.

Taking my phone, I open iTunes and begin to play *This Place* by Tamela Mann. I dig the hole and place the box inside.

Sweating and breathing hard, I kneel on the ground.

"Lord, your word says in Psalm 119:62, "At midnight I will rise to give thanks to You because of your righteous judgment." Thank you for never giving us what we deserve. Thank you, that even when we make mistakes, you still deem us worthy. And as I throw dirt on the box, ending this chapter of my life, I pray you will guide me into the next season that shall yield my rightful harvest. Amen."

I look at my watch and at 11:58, I begin to throw dirt until the box is covered.

At midnight, I say one last prayer, dust the dirt off my shoes and clothes, prop the shovel on the patio and go in the house.

After a shower, I grab my journal and climb into the bed.

September 1, 2018

Happy New Year to me.

I know it's not January, but I am claiming this as my New Year. Why? Because starting over means I am leaving everything that does not belong in the new, in the old. My marriage, it's in the old. Mistakes, it's in the old. Hurt and pain, it's in the old. All the stuff that did not survive in the old, I shall not replant in the new. I'm getting new seeds in order to reap new blessings that are mine and mine alone.

Happy New Year to me.

-- Signed, A New Me! ❤

I hope you have enjoyed The Marriage Bed. As with every book, my prayer is that you feel my heart. I don't know if you've ever dealt with trouble in your marriage or even if you are in the midst of a storm now but be quiet, this time and pray. Prayer has the power to usher you before God who is able to do all you need.

Trust Him.

Then, if you would, please leave a review and recommend it to your family and friends. And if there is anything you have questions on, email me.

As always, thank you! Words cannot express what it means to me each time you support me!

If this is your first time reading my work, please check out the many other books available by visiting my Amazon Page.

For upcoming contests and give-a-ways, I invite you to like my Facebook page, AuthorLakisha, follow my blog https://authorlakishajohnson.com/ or join my reading group Twins Write 2.

Or you can connect with me on Social Media.

Twitter: _kishajohnson | Instagram:

kishajohnson

Snapchat: Authorlakisha

Email: authorlakisha@gmail.com

About the Author

Lakisha Johnson, native Memphian and author of many titles was born to write. She'll tell you, "Writing didn't find me, it's was engraved in my spirit during creation." Along with being an author, she is an ordained minister, co-pastor, wife, mother and the product of a large family.

She is an avid social media poster and blogger at kishasdailydevotional.com where she utilizes her gifts to encourage others to tap into their God given talents. She won't claim to be the best at what she does nor does she have all the answers, she is simply grateful to be used by God.

Other Available Titles

A Secret Worth Keeping

A Secret Worth Keeping: Deleted Scenes

A Secret Worth Keeping 2

Ms. Nice Nasty

Ms. Nice Nasty: Cam's Confession

Ms. Nice Nasty 2

The Family That Lies

Dear God: Hear My Prayer

The Pastor's Admin

2:32AM: Losing Faith in God

The Forgotten Wife

Bible Chicks: Book 2

Doses of Devotion

You Only Live Once: Youth Devotional

HERoine Addict – Women's Journal

CPSIA information can be obtained
at www.ICGtesting.com
Printed in the USA
LVHW01s2104221018
594402LV00011B/1526/P

9 781720 105213